AS SEEN ON T.V.

John Wayne Comunale

For Uncle Charles, ya'll . . .

Other titles by John Wayne Comunale

ONE

Aᴿᵀᴵᴱ ᴡᴬᵀᶜᴴᴱᴰ ᵀᴴᴱ ᴡᴼᴹᴬᴺ ᴵᴺ front of him place her items on the counter, and he was trying hard, *really* hard, to keep his mouth shut. He'd been in line behind her at Bloomwalls drugstore for the last six minutes, eyeing what was in the small, red, plastic basket dangling from her liver-spotted claw of a hand. The wrinkly skin on her fingers hung loose like miniature scrotums except where it stretched tight over golf ball-sized knuckles swollen from years of arthritis.

The jiggly meat-bag woman had somehow manipulated the laws of physics by managing to slip two rings past her ball bearing knuckles. There were enough diamonds jammed into the gaudy baubles to pay off Artie's school loans but, of course, he'd stopped paying those some time ago. The sour-faced hag placed her final item on the counter, and Artie could hold his tongue no more.

"The new model is so worth it," he blurted out. "I mean, the original was good, but they've really outdone themselves with this new one."

He was, of course, talking about the Scrubtastic Extendable Scrub Stick she'd placed on the counter. It was marked with a label Artie knew very well, intimately even. It adorned many of the items in his home and contained the four best words in the English language: As Seen On T.V.

The cashier, whose name was Donna, was familiar with Artie's 'appreciation' for these products but offered no explanation to the beak-nosed bridge troll as to what he was referring. Donna wasn't the nicest person in the world and certainly had her moments of being what her ex-

1

husband referred to as a 'world-class bitch'. The only reason she tolerated Artie was because she thought he was mentally challenged or suffered a form of PTSD or both.

He, of course, was not, but often people didn't know what to make of his personality and assumed all sorts of things. Artie liked that his disposition could be perceived as disarming or annoying depending on who you asked and what time you asked them.

Unlike Donna, the bejeweled, elderly woman in front of Artie did not know of his penchant for the popular product line. Her back was to Artie, and she threw a quick half-glance over her shoulder, lips pursed tight like the first time, but she didn't acknowledge him. She gave Donna a look that said, *What's with this guy?*

Donna didn't particularly care if the woman found Artie annoying but only because she didn't care about anything having to do with her job, including the customers. To her, you were just a few ticks on the clock closer to quitting time. Donna stood stone-faced, staring straight ahead, mechanically moving items across a small piece of glass on the counter with a scanner beneath. She may as well have been a robot. The old woman opened her purse, stuck a scrotum-fingered hand inside, and waited for the total.

Artie thought himself tolerable of most behavior, and he was self-aware enough to know his quirks could wear people's patience thin, but one thing he could not tolerate was rudeness. There was just never a reason for it, and being rude was never helpful in *any* situation. Artie went out of his way to be polite to everyone, regardless of whether he knew them or not. This woman didn't know Artie from fuck-all, yet she deemed him unworthy of exchanging even a few words with.

The notion switched the track his train of thought was on, and he didn't realize it was his turn. Donna sighed longer than necessary before she called his name to snap him from the daze. Artie looked up just in time to see the old woman about to walk through the automatic door and called out to her.

"Well, I know you're gonna' love it." He smiled. "I liked it so much I had to get another one."

Artie held up the box he was holding. It was the same As Seen On

T.V. Scrubtastic Extendable Scrub Stick the woman had just purchased.

She paused at the door, mostly startled but also confused. Her wadded mash of a face shifted quickly to express annoyance as she stepped through the door with a huff, shaking her head all the way through the parking lot. Donna didn't see it, nor did anyone in line behind him, but Artie did.

It was barely perceptible, but this kind of thing never escaped his scrutinizing gaze.

It was fear.

In the slight moment between surprise and anger Artie saw fear clearly register on the old woman's face.

"Artie, for Christ's sake," said Donna, tapping her obnoxiously long, candy-purple colored fingernails on the counter. "People are waiting behind you."

Artie took one more moment to savor the delight the woman's fear had given him before turning around to face the line behind him. He put his hands up as if surrendering and stretched his mouth into an appealing smile.

"I'm sorry about that," he said, shaking his head. "So sorry, Donna."

Artie placed his item on the counter, took the basket from the hand of the woman behind him, and set it on the counter as well.

"To make up for it I'm going to pay for her items as well," said Artie, his smile never wavering.

"Oh no," said the woman, who was younger than Artie and had a toddler clutching her other hand. "It's really not that big of a deal. You don't need to do that."

"Ma'am, I'm sorry but I have to insist." Artie emptied the woman's basket on the counter so Donna could scan the contents. "I would feel awful for the rest of the week if I didn't. I assure you it's really my pleasure."

The woman acquiesced and her cheeks glowed red as she thanked him. It had been years since her husband had spoken that politely to her, and she had forgotten what it felt like.

When the transaction was finished Artie said goodbye to Donna and the woman and stepped out into the parking lot just in time to see a shit-brown Buick sedan pulling out into the street. Behind the wheel was the rude old woman.

TWO

ARTIE RAN HIS HURRICANE SPIN Brush across the black, ceramic tile of his bathroom floor for the fourth time in the last hour. He'd taken off and cleaned the easy to remove bristles twice already with the hose in the backyard and was going to have to do it at least one more time before he would be satisfied.

He'd redone his entire bathroom in black, including the sink, tub, and toilet, because it hid the blood better. The original white tile was too porous and turned pink within a month no matter how hard Artie scrubbed, so he switched everything out for their black counterparts. This helped conceal any mess, or at least made it less conspicuous, but Artie remained diligent in his cleaning.

How could he not with so many amazing cleaning products at his disposal thanks to the good people at As Seen On T.V.? Once he was satisfied with the floor he would move on to the walls and tub. Artie's As Seen On T.V. Hurricane Spin Scrubber With Extra Extension was leaned up against the wall next to the new Scrubtastic Extendable Scrub Stick he'd bought earlier that day. On the floor was the crumpled, bloody box of the Scrubtastic Extendable Scrub Stick old scrotum fingers had bought. Artie hadn't opened it yet, and hoped no damage was done to the product.

Between the three cleaning implements, he'd be able to get the bathroom floor, tub, and walls clean, but the small spatter in the corner of the ceiling was a different story. Artie had already gotten angry about it and thrown a fit, so there was no use in rehashing any more of that emotion.

This was just another one of those small learning experiences that happened from time to time, although they came with much less frequency these days. He thought he'd learned all the lessons he'd need to by now but was humble enough to acknowledge he benefitted from the ongoing learning experience.

Artie was confident something from his stable of Scrubtastic products would be able to remove the stain visually but nothing else. The blood was already in the microscopic holes of the drywall where it bound to the material in a way that made it impossible to fully clean. Artie was already brainstorming how he would cut the small section out and patch it without it being noticeable. He'd figure it out, he always did, but now he needed to focus on his task at hand.

The brushes whirred quietly, a feature he appreciated, and the soft sound acted like a white noise machine that soothed Artie. It helped slow down his mind, helped him to think. Cleaning had always been a cathartic experience, especially now more than ever, and he sometimes wondered if he was starting to enjoy cleaning more than killing, but that couldn't be true. He couldn't have one without the other, and either as a solitary act would be somehow less satisfying.

Artie flipped the switch on the handle to turn the device off and leaned it against the wall with the others. He would need to clean the brushes one more time, like he thought, but decided to start on the tub and walls before revisiting the floor. He plugged the drain and filled the tub with a few inches of hot water that turned red and murky as it mixed with castoff blood spatter.

Under the sink, Artie kept a variety of cleaning products, most of which were used to refill the reservoirs of various cleaning devices. He had to keep a few additional items on hand for when he had a particularly large mess to deal with like he did today. He pulled out a gallon bottle of bleach from the back and dumped half of it into the tub. Artie picked up the Scrubtastic brush closest to him, checked the tank to ensure it was filled with the exclusive, patented cleaning solution, and began to scrub his shower walls, ever so often dipping his bristles into the bleach water.

While he scrubbed, Artie's mind wandered back to a time when he had to clean up these kinds of messes without the help of As Seen On T.V. products. A mess like the one he was cleaning now would have taken at least three times longer, and even then it wouldn't be as clean as he could get things now.

The As Seen On T.V. Scrubtastic Scrub Stick was the first of such products he'd bought from Bloomwalls, but that was back before it was extendable. Artie used it to clean blood he'd tracked across the hardwood floor after a rather messy and complicated dispatching of a Boy Scout he'd lured from a campsite. Artie fell in love that day, and there was no going back. This was why he was excited to talk to the old woman about the one she was purchasing, because he knew she was going to love it. If she had only been kind enough to exchange a few words with him she would be at home right now, enjoying her scrub stick as much as Artie enjoyed his.

In hindsight, he was glad she had snubbed him, because it made Artie's decision for him. It was either going to be the old woman or the mother and child that had been behind him in line. Besides, it was always easier dealing with one person even if the second was only a kid. They had a tendency to slip through blood-slick hands and ended up being more trouble than they were worth.

It wasn't hard for Artie to snatch the old woman and get her back to his home. He easily caught up to the brown Buick, followed from a distance, and slowed to a crawl when it turned into a driveway. When the old woman got out of her car and opened the trunk to retrieve her bags, Artie made his move.

He swung into the driveway behind her, gave a light honk, and waved from the open driver-side window of his black Ford Tempo. It was the kind of car most people would refer to as a 'beater', but Artie was more concerned with having a vehicle that was inconspicuous rather than anything that might stand out in someone's mind.

"Excuse me, ma'am." Artie smiled as he stepped from the car. "It's me, the guy behind you in line at the Bloomwalls earlier. I asked you about your Scrubtastic Extendable Scrub Stick, remember?"

7

The woman seemed confused and thrown off guard as she looked down at the item he was talking about clutched in her hand. Artie closed his door and approached her, his hand behind his back concealing the blackjack he was holding. The blackjack was an antiquated weapon you don't typically hear about anymore, but that was why he liked it so much. It made him feel like he was being original by attempting to revive a fad in nineteenth-century weaponry.

He gave her time to respond as he closed the gap between them, but she remained tight-lipped and glared at Artie as he approached.

"I'm glad I was able to follow you because you dropped this when you walked out of the store. I wanted to make sure I gave it back to you."

"What's that?" she said, lowering her guard.

"This." Artie stepped up and clocked her in the side of the head with the leather-sacked hunk of lead.

He'd used the ancient weapon enough to know exactly how much force was needed to incapacitate and not kill. Her initial shock and confusion faded into sadness with the realization of what was happening. These expressions were priceless to Artie, and he often fell asleep to a cataloged slideshow of similar images he kept in his mind. Her knees buckled, and as she fell back into the trunk Artie slipped his arm around her back to guide her down.

He picked up her legs, swung them in, slammed the lid, and glanced around for witnesses. He'd scanned the area as he drove up already, but it never hurt to take a second look. He slipped the blackjack into his back pocket, placed his hands on the closed trunk, and breathed deeply, taking time to enjoy the moment.

The hard part was over and now Artie could work at his own pace, savoring every moment along the way. He walked around to the driver side of the old woman's car, reached through the open window, and pressed the button on a device attached to the visor. The garage door opened slowly, the rusty chain jerking the old wooden thing up against the ceiling.

Artie could tell from the sound of it there wasn't much life left in that chain, not that the old bag had to worry about it now. He climbed into the Buick and turned the key, conveniently still in the ignition. Artie hated having to dig through old women's purses because he usually ended up with two or three handfuls of used tissue and melted butterscotch before finding the keys, and that was if he was lucky.

He pulled the car into the garage, killed the engine, and left the key where he'd found it. Artie strolled out to his black Tempo, backed into the street, turned around, and backed it up the driveway, getting his bumper as close as he could to the Buick. When they were nearly touching, Artie popped his trunk, hopped out, then walked around to pop the Buick's trunk as well.

He transferred the woman to his trunk by leaning over the side and rolling her across the nearly touching bumpers. Artie slammed both trunks at the same time, moved his car down the driveway, and pulled the garage door down by the manual release. He'd come back later tonight to set a small 'accidental' fire, but that was hours from now. He would fill those hours 'dealing' with the old woman, and then he would clean to reflect and clear his head.

Now Artie dipped the Scrubtastic in the bloodied bleach water to take one more pass at the tiled walls around the tub before switching to his extendable Hurricane Brush to finish the job. Tomorrow, Artie would sleep most of the day, which was customary after a kill, but the day after tomorrow was Wednesday and he'd be up bright and early. This was the day the new As Seen On T.V. products went out on the shelves at Bloomwalls, and he planned on getting there when the doors opened.

THREE

Aʀᴛɪᴇ ᴡᴏᴋᴇ ᴡɪᴛʜ ᴀ ꜱᴛᴀʀᴛ from his post-kill sleep and swore he heard it again. He wasn't sure what *it* was he was hearing or if he was truly hearing anything at all. Whether it was in his head or not, the frequency with which he heard it was increasing.

The oddest thing was, for as many times as he'd heard—or thought he heard—the sound, he couldn't describe it. It was distinct and jarring, but when it yanked him from his sleep any concrete memory was lost along the way. No matter how hard he tried to hang on, the memory would dissolve into mist as soon he breached the surface of consciousness. He was starting to become concerned but hadn't fallen over the edge of panic just yet.

It was more than likely something as innocuous as the chirp of a smoke detector low on batteries. Not that exactly, but something like it. Artie was confident he would figure it out, and sooner rather than later, since it was happening more now.

The clock on the nightstand told Artie it was two hours earlier than he usually got up, but his mind had already begun to slowly churn with new thoughts. Ideas rolled around like rocks in a tumbler, spinning until they were smooth and polished. It was still dark outside, but Artie wasn't going back to sleep now.

He rolled from the warmth and comfort of the feather-down cocoon he'd been wrapped in for ten-plus hours, stepped into slippers, and walked across the very shiny, very polished hardwood floor. This was, of course, courtesy of Artie's Shiwala Spray Mop, another of his As Seen On T.V. favorites. At first he could never get his floors as shiny as the one on the infomercial, but then he figured out the magic formula of mixing the perfect proportions of wax and cleanser the device came with.

How to mix the chemicals was not included or suggested in the instructions, but Artie discovered this about many of his As Seen On T.V. products. They couldn't just come out and say how to achieve the *exact* results shown on the commercials because then anyone could do it. Artie particularly liked this 'speakeasy' aspect of the company, which he felt added an entire new level of depth to the products. Sure, the instructions would get you started but, to unlock the full potential of each product, you had to dig below the surface.

There was some guesswork and a decent amount of trial and error that went into this process each time, but the payoff was well worth it as far as Artie was concerned. Only truly devoted consumers, like Artie, were able to read between the lines to figure these things out. It was a point of pride for him.

Artie was completely nude save for his slippers. He caught a glimpse of himself in a full-length mirror just outside the kitchen. His physical appearance was also a point of pride for Artie, a pride even he could admit bordered on obsessive. He'd never been terribly overweight in his life but had suffered from body image issues since he was a child.

Growing up, Artie was a bit chubby, but not in a way other kids would pick on him or call him fat. In fact, Artie's weight wasn't even on the radar of his friends and classmates. They didn't notice the small, child-sized paunch of a stomach that made his Bugle Boy jeans harder and harder to button every time they came out of the dryer, but Artie noticed.

He couldn't help but notice and scrutinize the bodies of his peers, wishing to be more like them. The boys Artie played baseball with on the weekends were thin with no soft protrusions above their waistline like him. Some of the boys even had the faint beginning of muscle tone beginning to develop, which Artie coveted most of all. On the warmer days, most of the boys would play with their shirts off, but Artie would keep his on and deal with the heat and sweat.

During a time you weren't supposed to worry about anything except getting home for supper when the streetlights came on, Artie had given himself full-blown body dysmorphic disorder, and it still had its hooks in him to this day. He would try to starve himself by skipping meals at school and pocketing his lunch money. He would get up extra early some weekend mornings, sneak outside, and run around the block as many times as he could before any of his friends were up to question or judge his actions.

Artie hid these feelings from his parents because he felt shameful about not only his body but also his various attempts at getting in shape. This was the start of Artie bottling up the feelings he associated with shame and weakness. He hated this about himself. He didn't want to keep this all inside, but he lacked the ability to effectively communicate it to his parents.

At the beginning of the little league season, when Artie was ten, all the parents had to bring their kids to the VFW hall to be assigned to a team and pick up their uniforms. His father waited in the car as Artie followed some of the other boys inside and got in line. About ten minutes later Artie returned to the car clutching his uniform close to his chest and trying his damnedest to hold back tears.

He didn't say anything, but his father could tell by the redness of Artie's cheeks he was upset. When his dad asked what was wrong Artie said nothing, knowing if he tried to talk he wouldn't be able to keep from crying. His father pried further, demanding to know what was wrong. Artie couldn't hold back anymore and the tears began to flow as he attempted to explain.

Through tempered sobs he told his dad how the man in charge of passing out uniforms asked Artie what size jersey he wore, to which he had told the man large. He'd hoped to be in a medium this season, but he wasn't quite there yet. The man looked Artie up and down and said, "I think you better go with an extra large, kid." He couldn't protest even if he wanted because the lump leapt up into his throat before the man finished his sentence.

This made Artie's father angry, not with the man passing out uniforms, but with Artie for the way he reacted. The rest of the drive home, his father berated him for being too sensitive and told Artie he needed to toughen up if he was going to be worth half a shit when he was older. The tears stopped when they turned down their own street, and young Artie permanently locked away these feelings for the last time. They would no longer be shared with anyone and used only to torture himself with.

A few years later, when he hit puberty, his metabolism increased and he shot up another two feet, which helped flatten his belly and smooth out the love handles he'd had since he was six. He wouldn't let himself enjoy nature giving him exactly what he wanted though because he knew it was only a temporary solution. Even in his early teenage years Artie never lost sight of the work he would have to do for the rest of his life to maintain his desired body type.

He never let himself get swept up in the wave of carelessness that typically came with adolescence, another area of childhood he voluntarily opted out of. Being careless led to sharing too much of yourself, which was the last thing he wanted.

After the conversation with his father on uniform day and many similar subsequent conversations that followed, Artie only showed people what he wanted to show them. He became quite good at reading people and saying what he thought they expected him to say about himself.

Artie was very good at keeping everyone he knew at arm's length. He never allowed them to get too close, and therefore no one was ever able to call him on his bullshit. Not that anybody would because what little they knew about him they liked. Artie made sure of that. If he were to hand out business cards upon meeting someone it would list his occupation as 'Professional Acquaintance', because he was just that.

The people who knew Artie didn't really *know* Artie, which was exactly how he wanted it. It was a balancing act he'd spent his life mastering but well worth his time, since the only thing anyone could ever say about him was, "Artie? Yeah, I know him. Nice guy."

This was the opinion of anyone who knew or, rather, *thought* they knew, Artie, with 'nice' being the only adjective ever used to describe him. He was also aware when someone is revealed to have committed a horrible crime there's always an acquaintance or two on the news who say what a 'nice guy' the accused was. This wouldn't be the case for Artie though, because he would never be caught. He would maintain his 'nice guy' cred until the day he died.

Artie approved of what he saw in the brief glance he took at his reflection as he continued to the kitchen. His stomach wasn't flat; it was solid and contoured to showcase the muscle tone. Artie didn't like abs because he thought they were for dude-bros. He worked the muscles in his abdominal region to be sinewy yet subtle.

The kitchen light turned on automatically when he crossed over the threshold and his foot touched down on the tile. Artie had replaced the original tile with the same black ones he used for the bathroom floor. He used the kitchen while he was working from time to time, but the mess was such a bitch to clean up it almost wasn't worth it. Almost.

Artie had ripped the old, cheap tile out and treated the cement beneath with an acid/bleach combo he'd stumbled across during one of his many experiments with cleaning products. Artie found this particular combo ate the top layer off anything you applied it to, including concrete—a helpful discovery.

He didn't bring the old woman into the kitchen last night, so the tiles still gleamed with a showroom quality Artie strived to achieve. For this particular task, he used his As Seen On T.V. Spin-Maid Mop complete with dual, rotating brushes. Artie would soak each one overnight in a mixture of Dutch Glow Bathroom Tonic and My Cleaning Secret Extra Clean Fresh Gel, both important staples of Artie's improvised and experimental cleansers. One of his hall closets was dedicated to housing nothing but cases of the two products.

Artie pulled the stainless steel carafe from the base of his NuWave BrewHub coffee maker. The thing was programmed to kick on when an app on his cellphone detected Artie had woken up. It only worked about a third of the time, and this happened to be one of them. Artie honestly felt like the BrewHub was a piece of shit, but he was determined to stick with it, at least until the warranty went out. While the NuWave BrewHub wasn't an official As Seen On T.V. product, it was included under the umbrella of the company, so Artie felt beholden to the thing.

He hadn't ruled out the possibility the poor quality was intentional and the true potential of the machine was locked beneath the stainless sheath within the gears and wiring, like a puzzle. A puzzle the company expected him to solve if he indeed wanted his BrewHub to operate at optimal capacity, much like he had to do with finding the right mixture of cleaning chemicals.

Since he was up earlier than intended, Artie decided to fill the extra time with drinking coffee and exercising in the As Seen On T.V. Home Fitness Center and Health Arena he'd built out in his garage.

He didn't plan on putting clothes on to work out, and he sipped coffee from the brim of his mug while shuffling in his slippers toward the door to the garage. That was when he heard it. He heard the sound he'd been hearing in his dreams for weeks, only now he was awake. There was no doubt in his mind. It was the sound.

Just when he started to believe it may have been his imagination, Artie heard the sound again, loud, clear, and distinct. It came from somewhere on the right. He spun to face it and didn't know exactly what he was looking at.

There was something that looked like a bloated jack-o-lantern on the verge of melting into its own rotted rind pressed up against the lower pane of the living room window. Artie took a step closer to cut the glare from the glass and could now see it was actually a human face. A very fat, acne-covered, curly headed face. The face's thick lips twitched like two fat slugs fucking in a puddle of grease. Artie heard the sound again and, more than that, he saw it this time. The sound was coming from the lips of the hideous face.

FOUR

Aᴿᴛɪᴇ **DIDN'T CARE THAT HE** was naked. He wanted to know who the hell the face squished up against his window was attached to and why they were making *the* sound?

The thought occurred to Artie there was a strong possibility he might not actually be awake. He'd never heard the sound when he'd been awake before, so why should this time be any different? Now that he thought about it, the situation had all the classic earmarks of being a dream.

He was naked, after all, and the face *did* look twisted enough to be conjured from the stuff of nightmares. Artie was waiting for his mother to walk in topless with her head on backwards and hand him his high school diploma. Plus, he couldn't move. It was as if locking eyes with the individual looking into his window had somehow magnetized his feet to the floor.

The chubby, wet lips twitched again in perfect sync with the sound. Artie flinched, sloshing lukewarm coffee over the edge of his mug to splash on the floor between his feet. When the droplets hit his ankle Artie realized he actually wasn't magnetized to the floor, and while he had thought he might be dreaming, he now knew he wasn't. Artie was no longer chasing the sound through a tunnel from sleep to awake.

He could distinctly tell it was actually like a combination of three sounds balanced together in a way that made it wholly unique. It sounded like the ugly face stuck to the window was clearing its throat while hacking up a wet cough combined with an even wetter sneeze. It was disgusting.

Artie cleared the distance to the window in three fast, long strides. He still held the half empty mug in one hand and reached out toward the window with the other. The face disengaged from the glass just as Artie's fingers touched the pane, leaving behind a calling card of greasy, translucent sludge. Artie threw open the window, knowing he'd have to use several applications of Full Crystal Window Cleaner to restore its clarity.

He hadn't thought much past opening the window, so as the person with the face stumbled backward, Artie threw his coffee at him, quickly followed by the mug for good measure. The tepid, bitter brew splashed the person in the face a second before the mug made contact with a wide, slightly sloped forehead. Stubby fingers attached to chubby hands covered the face while warm-ish coffee sputtered between fat, wet lips. Artie was fuming, but he took a breath and stayed himself before doing something rude like scream in this person's face.

"Excuse me." Artie cleared his throat and leaned out the open window. "Can I help you, or are you just looking?"

Artie was proud of himself for asking politely while slipping a joke in as well. A joke the person bent over with their head in their hands, moaning, probably wasn't paying attention to. Not that they would appreciate it given the circumstances. However, given that Artie was naked added a layer of innuendo to an already solid quip.

"My head," moaned the odd man whose face was just pressed against Artie's window. "My head, my head, my head, my head."

Artie's patience was being tested again, but he let the injured voyeur finish bemoaning his pain before addressing him again. Artie spoke when the only sound coming from the person was labored breaths on the verge of sobs.

"I hope you know you deserved worse than that," Artie started. "Now, tell me who you are, what you're doing, and how long you've been making that . . . sound with your mouth?"

Fat fingers slipped away from the face, and Artie could see it clearly for the first time. There was no question now that this person was male, but his age was indeterminable. In the face he appeared a typical, pimple-faced, chubby-cheeked, dick-jerkin' teenager, but his body was blown up and disproportionate. He didn't look grown up but literally *blown up*, like someone had stuck an air compressor hose in his asshole, turned it on, and walked away, making him into the hideous, miniature, parade balloon-like reject before him.

"I'm . . . I'm your neighbor," stuttered the man raising his eyes to meet Artie's.

"Ms. Lancaster is my neighbor," answered Artie. "Are you one of her relatives or something?"

"No. I moved into the garage apartment."

The man went back to rubbing his forehead. Artie was far enough away to not see the colony of zits being ruptured as the stranger vigorously rubbed the spot where the coffee mug struck, but he could hear them. A muted snap sounded each time the skin stretched tight enough over a whitehead to pop out its slimy discharge, causing the man's head to glisten even brighter in the moonlight.

"I wasn't aware she was renting out the room," said Artie, mostly to hear something other than tiny, exploding lesions.

"Uhhnwo?" The man shrugged his shoulders.

"And why is it you were attempting to make your face one with my window again?"

"You sleep a lot," said the man.

Artie balked at this remark. He wanted to think he was prepared to hear an array of bullshit excuses spout from the man's chubby meat-flaps and felt he himself was equally equipped with an abundance of retorts, but this was not an answer he was prepared for. It wasn't even an answer.

Artie's demeanor darkened as he realized he might not be dealing with a run-of-the-mill peeping tom. He repositioned himself for a quick retreat back from the window in case the strange man-boy decided to launch a surprise attack.

"Why are you looking in my window?" Artie's tone went cold and stern.

The man pursed his lips into a caricaturist pout and stared up at

18

Artie. He sniveled and snorted like he was breathing through a wet sponge in lieu of a verbal response. He dropped his hands to his side, clenching and unclenching his fingers over and over like he couldn't decide if he wanted to make a fist or not. His expression adjusted slightly to reflect a growing anger inside of him. His snivels and snorts turned to heavy panting before falling into a slow and steady hypnotic rhythm.

"I'm going to ask you one more time," said Artie. "Why are you lo—"

The man suddenly charged the window, his fists clenched, screaming like a mad man rushing voluntarily to his demise. Artie was surprised, but his instinct and reflexes were far too keen for him to be taken down by such an attack. After the first few years of killing clumsily, he was at the point of being able to anticipate and either dodge or counter almost any attack, this, of course, being no exception.

He'd learned over the years to conserve his energy during a confrontation and use his surroundings to his benefit, so Artie pulled back out of the window and stepped to the side. He expected the man to run headlong into the side of the house, but the greasy-faced bastard actually leapt high enough to fly right through the open window as if Artie were a naked and cape-less matador. The man's arms were outstretched in a fat, sloppy Superman impression with his hands open and ready to clamp around Artie's neck.

The man's attempt at flight was short-lived, and the plump peeper flew just far enough to clear the sill before smacking against the hardwood floor beer-belly first. The sound of soft, blubbery under-flesh slapping the floor bounced around the minimalistic décor of Artie's living room and echoed through the otherwise silent house. Momentum carried the man down the slick, polished floor on his belly, leaving a human-sized, greasy snail-trail behind.

He kept going until his head hit drywall, which collapsed upon impact with a hollow crunch. If the wall hadn't stopped him he could have easily slid another five or six feet. There was a beat of silence between the two men in which Artie decided how to handle this problem. Moans of pain were pushing their way past sickeningly thick, wet lips before Artie was upon him.

He pulled the man's head back by a handful of mangy, oily curls and dug his left knee into the center of the stranger's spine. Artie applied firm pressure to force the air from the man's lungs while pulling his neck up to prevent him from drawing another breath. Artie used this particular way of disabling his more spirited kills, and his movements were smooth and practiced.

Then, something went wrong.

The hair of the pimple-faced, fat intruder was too slick and slipped slowly through Artie's fingers. He adjusted his grip, allowing the man to suck in half a breath, but he still couldn't hold on. It was like the son-of-a-bitch had been dunked into a vat of cooking grease.

Artie let go of the sickeningly slick curls and pushed down on the back of the man's head instead, forcing the fat, monstrous face into the floor lips first. Artie kept his knee pressed in the stranger's back and used both hands to grab his ears. He pulled up then slammed the fat head into the floor again and again and, while the ears were just as slimy as the man's hair, Artie kept a firm grip by digging his nails into the meaty cartilage. The ears were deformed by fat, and it felt like he was holding two raw, lukewarm, rubbery chicken cutlets. Also, the man's ears secreted a substance thicker than the grease in his hair and, as he squeezed, Artie felt like he was ringing tapioca out of sponges.

Artie had no idea who this person was or how the situation had escalated to this, but he was quite good at thinking on his feet. The man stopped what little struggling he had been attempting, and the moans tapered off into shallow, wet, labored breaths. Artie climbed off the man's back, stood up, and cringed at the realization that his naked dick and balls had just been pressed against a t-shirt soaked through with sweat and the industrial strength lube the man secreted. Artie held his arms out away from his body, wanting to wipe himself off without using his bare hands. He kicked the man in the side of his fat gut in frustration, launching a mist of the toxic mixture up from the point of impact.

Artie didn't want to believe that a few of the poisonous droplets had entered his partially open mouth, but his taste buds told him otherwise. His brain could only best process it as body odor made into a flavor. The vileness attacked his tongue like it was being tattooed by hundreds of inked-up needles permanently scarring their way from one side to the other.

He looked down at the pudgy, moist, cartoonish man and spat furiously on the back of his head, attempting to return the awful taste back to where it came from. Artie spat until his mouth was desert dry, and even then he still tried to will saliva from overworked glands.

Satisfied, Artie took a step toward the kitchen to get a towel and a glass of sparkling water from his Bubble Yourself Home Carbonation Unit, but he noticed something and stopped. The sloppy gurgling noises coming from the man had ceased, leaving Artie in complete silence for the first time since he opened the window. He looked at the pitiful, lumpy body on the floor before him and noticed that wasn't the only thing that had stopped.

The steady rise and fall of the man's midsection was stuck in the down position. The fat fuck had stopped breathing. This wasn't exactly how Artie wanted this to go down, but here he was and he would deal with it. He got on his knees next to the man's head and went to take hold of the grease-slicked, tangled curls one more time so he could turn the man's face toward him.

Then, the head moved. More specifically, it jumped. It jumped right up into Artie's hand before he'd lowered it enough to grab hold himself.

Artie let go and backed away on his knees, but the head remained suspended an inch or so off the floor and began to rotate slowly. As the head turned, more of the face was revealed to Artie, allowing him to see the damage he'd done to it with the floor. Both eyes were bloodied and swollen shut while misshapen globs of bruised tissue sprung up all around them.

The nose was smashed flat and spread wide across the center of his face, which was wet and shiny with pus from all the pimples popped in the process. Thick, milky fluid thinned by blood flowed freely down fat cheeks like tiny, pink waterfalls. It could almost be considered a breathtaking sight if you didn't know what you were looking at.

Pimple pus wormed its way through cracks cut deep across blood-engorged lips, swollen as if to purposely accentuate their cartoonish quality. Artie swore he saw a slight tremble work its way diagonally down the lips. It was so subtle he was sure he'd imagined it but it happened again, and then again until they were twitching like electric current had been shot through them.

Small slits appeared across the swollen tissue covering the top portion of the man's face and fell open on each side, exposing eyeballs hiding beneath. Within the same moment, the lips twisted in the way Artie had seen earlier, followed immediately by the dreaded sound.

Artie flinched as the sound leapt into his head and chewed a trench across it like blades tilling a field. He rocked on his knees, lost his balance, and fell backward. Artie flung his hands behind him, hoping to somewhat break his fall, but the floor was gone now and he just kept falling.

The alarm on Artie's nightstand bleated like a lamb being marched to slaughter, and he opened his eyes.

FIVE

ARTIE LAY STILL IN BED and let his alarm clock continue to go off for thirty more seconds. He was groggy and confused and not entirely sure what was real at the moment. Artie reached out and lightly tapped the top of the As Seen On T.V. combination alarm clock, white noise machine, and sleep pattern analyzer cleverly dubbed the Snooze-A-Tron Sleep Mate. He slowly pulled himself up into a seated position and massaged the bridge of his nose between his thumb and forefinger. When he closed his eyes he saw the man's face, but not actually the face as much as the lips.

Could the whole thing have been a dream? He asked himself the question rhetorically, already knowing there was no other explanation. Artie tried to grasp at specific memories from the dream, but they turned to smoke in his hand and disappeared one by one. The only thing he could recall was the image of those lips like two obese snails outgrowing their shells and trying to burrow into each other for warmth.

Artie remembered the lips had been responsible for the sound and, despite having heard it several times in the dream, any memory of it eluded him. He had an idea, or at least he thought he did, but no matter how hard Artie concentrated he couldn't drag the sound's description from the bottomless pit of his subconscious.

He rolled from his bed and stepped into slippers waiting to swallow his feet in soft, warm sheepskin lining. Artie didn't usually keep items that belonged to his victims. It was way too risky, and he didn't understand the mentality behind keeping a 'trophy' from every kill. Doing that upped the chances, or pretty much guaranteed, you would be caught eventually. Artie didn't want to be caught, and keeping mementos to feed his ego wasn't worth being forcefully made to stop.

The slippers had been the one exception he'd made. They were unused and wrapped in a plastic bag when he found them stuffed beneath other random items in the trunk of one of his victims from years back. It appeared they were going to be given to someone as a gift so, before Artie ditched the car, he decided to graciously accept them on behalf of whomever they had been meant for. He didn't regret the decision.

By the time Artie walked the ten feet from his bed to the bathroom he'd almost all but forgotten about the dream, and as he brushed his teeth with his three-speed Sparkle Ultra Electric Toothbrush it was out of his mind completely. He was focused on getting over to Bloomwalls and unwilling to dedicate precious mindshare to dream analysis.

Once dressed, a shrill beep sounded from the kitchen, telling him the BrewHub had completed brewing his coffee right on time, just as he'd programmed it to. He tied his shoes and headed to the kitchen to pour a cup for the road before getting on his way.

He used to stay up late the night before the new As Seen On T.V. products came out to research all the new models and specs but found if he already knew everything about what was being released he would just walk into the store, pick up the items, purchase them, and be back in his car in less than ten minutes. It was an efficient practice, sure, but Artie quickly figured out he enjoyed the ritual of the discovery just as much as he did the products themselves.

He now went in blind and would spend hours in the As Seen On T.V. aisle poring over every bit of text on each box while randomly exclaiming things out loud to himself like, *Unbelievable* or *That's incredible,* and, of course, *This is too good to be true.* The employees of Bloomwalls, especially Donna, dreaded these visits from Artie but, lucky for them, they never let on how it bothered them.

Artie crossed the threshold from the hallway into the living room and froze. He'd experienced déjà vu before, or at least what he thought was déjà vu, but the feeling had never been strong enough to stop him in his tracks. His equilibrium momentarily shifted when the image flashed across his mind's eye, and Artie leaned against the wall to steady himself.

The image was intense but fleeting, leaving only a vague impression of what he'd seen and was translated to a feeling of familiar discomfort. He thought he remembered his dream having something to do with the living room but, beyond that, he drew a blank.

Artie cleared his mind and let the creepy feeling wash away with thoughts of his task at hand. He'd wasted enough time dwelling on dream nonsense and hurried across the living room to grab his coffee from the kitchen.

He stopped just before stepping onto the dark tiles of the kitchen and swore what he saw was a trick of the light shining through the window across the floor. He still needed to turn around and take a second look just to reassure himself the reflected sunlight was indeed responsible. What he thought he'd seen was a section of floor about two feet wide and stretching the length of the room that appeared lighter in color than the wood on either side. Like it had been bleached or sanded.

Artie stepped over to the area in question with his back blocking the sunlight from the window. With his shadow cast across the floor Artie could tell it was indeed the light creating the illusion. Satisfied, he continued to the kitchen but stopped short again when something else caught his eye.

He saw it on the floor a few inches from the wall in front of him but couldn't tell what it was from where he stood. It was small, dark, and possibly round, and three steps later, when he stood over it, there was no confusion as to what it was.

Blood.

A small, perfectly round drop of dried blood the size of a dime dotted the otherwise spotless floor. Artie stared down at the spot, attempting to make sense of it. His face grew warm and then hot and then boiling, until tiny drops of perspiration splashed against the floor, dotting the area around the blood.

SIX

ARTIE SPED DOWN SYCAMORE STREET, rolled the stop sign, and accelerated through the turn onto Bradley Boulevard. He'd wasted too much time staring down at the floor, backtracking his every move from the night before, trying to figure out exactly how it was possible for a drop of blood to make its way to his living room.

He was always especially careful and calculated in every move he made, particularly within his own house where he was in full and complete control. Aside from the occasional kitchen, kill blood was relegated to two parts of Artie's home, the first being the bathroom, which he labored over, scrubbing spotlessly clean after each kill. The second was an extra bedroom at the end of the hall he playfully dubbed the 'killing floor'. Artie did most of his best work in that room.

He was diligent in keeping blood and all other bodily fluids in those two areas only. He even had specific hampers lined with industrial strength plastic bags like the kind they used on construction sites to clean up the smaller chunks of debris. They were six millimeters thick, as opposed to the conventional two, and were specially made to be non-porous for the purpose of keeping even the smallest of dust particles from escaping, just in case they were used for cleaning up asbestos, fiberglass insulation, or anything else that could be considered hazardous.

This meant they also kept fluids, like blood for instance, from leaking through, and the strength of the thickness kept the bag from being pierced by something like a broken 2x4 or the jagged end of a snapped femur. They were one of very few items not affiliated with the As Seen On T.V. brand Artie used, but they were necessary.

The small, perfectly round droplet of mystery blood vexed Artie no matter how hard he tried to put it out of his mind by distracting himself with thoughts of new As Seen On T.V. products he was currently exceeding the speed limit by twenty-plus miles per hour to obtain.

The blood had mostly dried and was a shade of crimson so deep it was almost black. Not quite black yet but almost, which was the most troubling for Artie. He wasn't formally trained, but he'd had enough 'hands on' experience with blood to know a thing or two. The particular stage of drying in which Artie found the drop on his floor meant it had more than likely been deposited there sometime between three and four hours before being discovered.

Artie expected a forgotten memory of the night prior to suddenly emerge from his subconscious and explain exactly how the blood got there. Whether it did or didn't, he'd left the droplet on the floor undisturbed to further scrutinize when he got back home.

He swung into the Bloomwalls parking lot, only lightly applying his brakes, and the back end of his decade-old Toyota Corolla fishtailed across patches of gravel on the otherwise smooth asphalt. Artie used the wheel to fight the centrifugal force and straighten the vehicle out as he pointed it toward a parking space, slammed the brakes, and skid to a stop between two white lines. Artie was flustered, which proved to be more of a distraction than he cared for.

He gripped the door handle, paused to take a deep breath, and reset his mind yet another time. He needed to remind himself not to dwell on things he had no control over, which was nearly impossible due to the control complex he'd not only dealt with his whole life but had also fostered to grow and strengthen.

When he got home he'd have plenty of time to figure out how and why the blood was in the living room, and likely discover such an obvious answer he would feel foolish for not thinking of it earlier. The thought of this hypothesized outcome was enough to send some much needed ease through Artie's rattled being. He popped the door open and leapt out of the car, smiling wide as he made a beeline for the entrance.

The automatic door was almost too slow, but Artie slid through the narrow opening sideways, without slowing his pace. The store was quiet, as it usually was in the morning, and although they'd only been open fifteen minutes Artie felt like he was running hours behind. He was usually the first one through the door on days new As Seen On T.V. items were released and would even stop to pick up a coffee for Donna, handing it to her when she unlocked the door and let him in.

She always accepted the coffee, but she never said thank you. At first, Artie perceived this behavior as extremely rude, and Donna ended up at the top of his list for a few weeks until he realized this was just the way she was. After several days in a row of coming to Bloomwalls first thing in the morning to observe Donna's routine and find the most convenient time to snatch her up, he observed her communicating with only nods and grunts until at least eleven a.m. Since she wasn't directing this behavior solely at Artie, he let go of his hostility for her, chalking it up to being a part of her uniquely frigid personality.

Artie hurried past the counter where Donna was leaning against the cash register flipping through a fashion magazine. She didn't look up or acknowledge him, but she would've done the same regardless of who walked in, so Artie didn't take offense.

"Morning, Donna," he sang, trying to sound cheery without letting frustration bleed into his tone.

She said nothing in response, as he'd expected, and he continued down to the aisle his feet couldn't seem to get him to fast enough. Artie observed several older ladies from the neighborhood—blue-hairs, as he called them—standing in the aisles he passed on his way. They did nothing but shamble up and down each aisle behind a full-sized shopping cart in which they deposited one or sometimes as many as two items at a time. They were like animatronic props running on a track, locking them forever in routine. It irked Artie that the blue-hairs had gotten to the store before him, but it all went away when he reached his aisle. The smell hit him first. The unique aroma new As Seen On T.V. products gave off when put on the shelf was intoxicating to Artie.

Some might attribute the smell to 'off-gassing', which is the dissipation of chemicals used in production of the items, but he didn't see it that way. To Artie, he smelled the hidden magic bestowed on each and every product the company put out. He smelled the secret waiting to be unlocked within the items, taunting him to figure it out. Artie paused at the start of the aisle to take several deep breaths. His head swam in the excess endorphins dumped from his brain, one of the desired effects of the scent.

He reached out for a nearby shelf to steady himself as the euphoria ebbed to a level at which he could operate. He took a breath, held it for a moment, and closed his eyes. The irritation he felt from dwelling on his odd dream, along with the anxiety of having to deal with the drop of blood in his living room, melted away in that moment, allowing his mind to be occupied only by the task at hand.

When he opened his eyes he found himself face-to-face with one of the aisle-rambling blue-hairs. She had stopped her cart three inches from Artie and stood at the other end, scowling while she gripped the handle with the intensity of a captain fighting to keep his ship afloat in a typhoon. Her bulging knuckles were extra white due to thin and withered skin pulled tight across arthritic bone. Artie maintained eye contact and smiled to disarm the old woman.

"Excuse me. I'm so sorry. I guess I got caught up in a daydream there for a second. Please accept my apology."

Artie spoke with a saccharine sweetness typically found two aisles over in the excessive amount of candy associated with whatever the closest upcoming holiday was. He stepped to the side and gave an exaggerated wave, gesturing for the woman to pass by. She pushed a single grunt through stubbly, sourpuss lips in response and shambled past Artie muttering something about *dopers* and *syphilis.*

As off-putting as the behavior of this woman was, Artie remained unaffected. He was already late and didn't want to waste any more time not basking in the presence of the newest products guaranteed to make his life easier.

He turned to face the right side of the aisle, which was the only side he needed concern himself with. The other side contained a small selection of office supplies, pens, markers, and batteries for everything from a watch to an industrial flashlight.

The first items displayed at the start of the aisle were left from the collection prior. The far opposite end of the aisle was organized in the same way to make room for the factory fresh, brand-spankin' new models from the geniuses behind As Seen On T.V. The center shelf space was highly coveted and reserved for only the newest of items.

Artie took his time looking over items released the month prior, despite having owned them since they'd been released thirty days ago. Still, he was always looking for something he might have missed. He wouldn't be able to live with himself if he'd accidentally missed out on a product that had been discontinued. This also helped build the anticipation, and he took his time to savor the feeling. He wasn't a selfish lover and recognized the intimate push/pull of the experience. Artie would push just as good as he got pulled.

When he reached the center section, he stopped in front of each new product individually, picked up the box, and read every bit of information printed on it. Artie would not let his eyes wander any farther down the shelf so as to preserve the mystery of what was to come next, allowing him to be pleasantly surprised every time.

The nature of the surprise remained pleasant for the first two new items he saw but quickly nosedived into very non-pleasant territory. The first item Artie examined was called The Airpop Wireless Popcorn Thermostat, which the box claimed would make perfect, fluffy popcorn using only hot air while also controlling your home's thermostat to your pre-programmed specifications. Artie wondered why so many products incorporated a popcorn maker as part of them, but he knew there were people at As Seen On T.V. whose job it was to know exactly why, which was good enough for him.

The second new item displayed was the Space Ace Shelf Space Spacer (with optional Airpop Popcorn Maker attachment). As far as Artie could tell, the device was primarily used for creating space in linen closets, particularly where sheets were concerned. The box claimed the item utilized a patented, revolutionary automatic folding device that reduced the size of folded sheets by fifty percent. Artie himself only had two sets of sheets, but he could still see the value in owning such a thing.

Artie took another step down the aisle but, instead of finding the next new product in front of him, he found a gap. He could see the next product down the line in his peripheral but, before that and after the Space Spacer, there was . . . well, there was a space. A tag attached to the shelf below the empty gap showed there had indeed been something there and that something cost twenty-nine ninety-five.

Artie moved closer to the tag so he could read the small print below the price describing the product. It said:

As Seen On T.V. Greaseless Hair De-Greaser, Straightener, and Popcorn Maker.

SEVEN

DONNA HAD BEEN NO HELP, which wasn't unusual, so Artie couldn't be that upset. He was actually extremely upset but didn't want Donna to pick up on the intensity with which he was experiencing the emotion. Not that he was in any danger of Donna picking up anything that wasn't the newest issue of whatever innocuous fashion magazine to come out that week.

Artie tried to get as much information about who had gotten to the store before him and bought the entire inventory of the one new product absent from the shelf. At first, she claimed she didn't know what he was talking about as she flipped the glossy pages of the magazine on the counter in front of her.

Donna hadn't bothered to look up long enough to make eye contact with Artie during his query, which was off-putting, but he was unaffected at the moment. He had too many unknowns floating around in his brain to be offended by the gruff and stoic attitude of the cashier.

"You were the first one here like always, Artie," Donna said while her eyes scanned over words describing the do's and don'ts of this year's cocktail hour attire. "I unlocked the door and let you in myself, remember? You gave me coffee."

Donna gestured to the area next to her register where the cup of coffee Artie usually brought her would have been perched, but the space was empty.

"I think you might be confused, Donna," Artie said, doing his best to keep the anxious waver out of his voice. "I wasn't the first one here today. I . . . I overslept and was running late."

Donna reached out to grab the nonexistent cup of coffee without looking up from her magazine and closed her fingers around thin air. She opened and closed her fingers three more times before finally looking up, clearly confused and annoyed.

"Where'd my coffee go? Did you move it or something?"

Donna looked around the register, under the counter, behind her on the cigarette shelf, and even checked underneath her magazine as if something could be hidden there.

"Donna, look," said Artie, putting both hands on the counter and leaning in closer, "you're thinking of last month when I came in and brought you coffee. I wasn't the first one here today, but I need you to tell me who came in before me and bought all of the new As Seen On T.V. Greaseless Hair De-Greaser, Straightener, and Popcorn Makers?!?"

Artie had tried not to raise his voice, but found himself yelling by the end of his question. Donna squinted and wrinkled her nose, wiggling it back and forth, breathing heavy and loud as she examined Artie up and down.

"I guess it wasn't you who came in first today."

Donna nodded, affirming her own statement, then turned her eyes back down to the magazine. Artie had never known a person as unattached and dissociative as Donna, and he envied her for that. He paused to let a beat pass between them to try and reset the tone of their conversation.

"Do you happen to remember the person who *did* come in early, and perhaps made a large purchase? Maybe they were buying several of the same item?"

Artie's tone was relaxed and casual as he spoke, now trying to come off as nonchalant as possible. Instead of a desperate lunatic demanding information, he now seemed like he was making casual conversation with an old friend.

"Now that I think about it," said Donna, actually lifting her head when she spoke. "There was this old lady who came in earlier and bought some things."

"Oh really? Do you know who she was, or—I mean was she a regular?"

"I think she might ha—" Donna stopped short, focusing on something over Artie's shoulder. "Oh, never mind. There she is right there."

Artie swiveled around to see the old woman he'd encountered earlier in the aisle. She looked back at Artie with a wild hatred in her eyes and gave him the finger before disappearing into an aisle. When he turned back around, Donna had her nose buried in her magazine again.

"Can you remember anybody else that may have come in? Anyone else at all that's not me or that old woman?"

"Maybe," she said, licking her finger before turning a page. "Maybe . . . I'm not sure if I ca—"

"Excuse me, young man," came a voice from Artie's left. "Are you just going to chat it up all day?"

He turned to see one of the roaming blue-hairs now waiting in line behind him. When he took a step back Artie saw there were three more of them behind her. The only one missing was the charmer who'd just given him the finger.

"I'm sorry about that," Artie started. "I just need to get some inf—"

"Sorry, Artie," Donna said, pushing her magazine to the side. "I've got customers. I'll help you find whatever you lost later."

"But I didn't lose anything! I need to know who wa—"

The blue-hair stepped in front of him before he could finish and edged him out farther with her ample sized rear-end. Artie gave up on Donna for now and went back to the As Seen On T.V. aisle to take another look.

EIGHT

ARTIE DROVE HOME FROM BLOOMWALLS more frustrated than before he'd gotten there. He barely retained flashes of the odd dream from the prior night and, while what he could recall made no sense, he couldn't stop thinking about it. Artie had a strange feeling he was hoping to bury beneath an avalanche of logic. He didn't want to believe it but couldn't stop coming back around to the thought the missing product, the drop of blood on his floor, and the dream were all related. It was crazy and not at all like Artie to believe something like that, but the fact he was entertaining the idea was troubling in itself.

He decided he needed a hard reset to the day, much like he'd tried to reset his interaction with Donna earlier. From the second Artie opened his eyes that morning he'd been propelled by uncontrollable chaos. The dream left his consciousness covered in residue like a slimy infant pulled straight from the birth canal and, no matter how hard he tried to scrub himself of it mentally, there were still moist and tacky patches left over.

Artie had been knocked off-kilter by the dream coupled with the drop of blood, but the gap in the shelf at Bloomwalls was almost too much. One after another, these things hit like a boxer's three-punch combo. Artie could feel himself falling backward and hoped the ropes against his back would be enough to keep him upright.

The back seat of his car was filled with boxes of each new As Seen On T.V. product sans the one missing. Artie bought two of some of the items, already anticipating where he would most need to use them in his home, and you never knew where you were going to have to control your thermostat from. Plus, he'd need to disassemble some of them in order to unlock their secret use, and he usually destroyed a few items in the process.

In Artie's trunk was the unconscious body of a young male panhandler who'd been holding a sign at the corner for the last four days that said: *Need Money for Weed and Beer. The Children are our Future. God Bless.* The humor of the sign wasn't lost on Artie. He appreciated the sentiment of the sign and respected anyone's ability to laugh in the face of hard times, but this particular man and his sign had bothered him the past four days.

Artie himself had been down on his luck during certain times in his life, so he understood how someone's life could change drastically in an instant. When he first saw the man, Artie thought back to a time when he was just a pussy hair away from standing with a sign and cup at the busy intersection. This was the only time in his life when he stole from his victims and for only a very brief period, until he was able to get back on his feet.

Artie didn't get the point of stealing and, quite frankly, felt it was beneath him. Thieves steal things and get rid of them as fast as they can in order to get money, which they then spend as fast as they can. They take no time to relish in what they've done. They get no satisfaction out of it other than the temporary adrenaline dump, and that's not even as great as they make it sound in the movies.

When Artie killed, he felt something. There was a satisfaction in what he did, but there was something else that came with it. An intangible energy Artie would carry around inside and feed off, trying to make it last a little longer each time. Thieves didn't feel things like this because they were opportunistic and shallow. And besides, stealing from someone was quite rude.

Artie equated the young man with the sign to a thief because he was most certainly able-bodied, and his homelessness came off as a choice, not a last resort. He'd more than likely got into some 'you can't tell me what to do, I'll show you' type of argument with his perfectly reasonable, well-meaning parents, and his rebellion of the week became panhandling, not for money to live off of, but for booze and dope.

The young man was using false hardship like a weapon in a stick-up, which worked like a charm on a certain type of people susceptible to that sort of thing. Exploiting kindness was a form of ill-mannered behavior Artie couldn't abide, so he decided to pick the kid up. Artie rolled his window down and asked if the kid wanted to jump in the car and smoke a joint then go find a party.

He didn't hesitate to leap in, too excited and aloof to sense danger, and when they turned the corner his forehead smacked the dashboard from the force of the blackjack striking the back of his skull. The confused wannabe vagrant sunk in is seat as consciousness closed up around him like he was being tied up in a sack. Artie had pulled the car over behind a closed down tire shop a block up from the corner and moved the unconscious body to his trunk.

He didn't consider himself a Samaritan, nor did he think he was doing a service to anyone by removing an entitled, lazy lump of a person from society. His motivation for killing was always selfish and personal. The justifications he made were like tiny weights that balanced out the scale of his sanity.

Artie sped through the turn onto his street, his mind bouncing back and forth from thoughts of killing the young man in his trunk to trying all the new As Seen On T.V. products strewn across his backseat. He would have to deal with the lazy panhandler first, of course, but then his mind and body would be completely at ease and balanced. He would get even more enjoyment out of experimenting with his new toys despite the glaring fact he was one short of completing the new product line.

While it wouldn't be easy, Artie could wait until Bloomwalls restocked to obtain the missing item, but he still planned to grill Donna daily for more information on who this mystery customer was. He couldn't shake the eerie feeling that had hold of him since he woke up and couldn't wait for the solace he'd achieve by killing the man in his trunk.

Artie slowed as he approached his house and made the long, lazy right into his driveway. He noticed something to his left as the front tires bounced gently over the threshold of the immaculately smooth pavement he'd painstakingly installed himself. He glanced and saw the something was a someone, and that someone was watering the potted plants in front of Ms. Lancaster's garage apartment.

It was hard for Artie to tell if it was a man or a woman at this distance, mostly due to the person's bulbous, bloated body. When he got closer he saw it was a man, albeit an unconventional looking man. His cheeks were cartoonishly exaggerated, and his whole face was marred by a catastrophic amount of acne. Sweat mixed with the grease pumping out of his pores to create a sheen that glistened blindingly in the midday sun.

Another odd feature was the man's hair. It wasn't the greasy mess you would assume came with the kind of face it sat above but, in fact, quite the opposite. The black hair plunged in an aggressively straight line from the man's fat head down to his shoulders with the silky luster of a shampoo commercial model. The hair was healthy, clean, and what some would describe as gorgeous, but was so straight it looked unnatural. It was as if this man's hair existed within the uncanny valley, causing Artie's brain to tell his eyes to call bullshit.

The man's hair barely moved, shifting only slightly as he went from plant to plant dipping an old style green, metal watering can down toward each pot until the sufficient amount of water was poured. The hair was too real looking to be fake and too absurd to be real, but either way, it was firmly affixed to the strange man's head.

The automatic garage door opener initiated as Artie approached, and as he was about to pull in, the man stopped watering, looked up, and turned to face him. Artie slowed the car to meet his gaze and noticed a purplish-black lump jutting from the center of his forehead like a deformed unicorn horn. The man squinted, trying to get a better look at Artie, but then smiled and waved like they had been neighbors their whole lives.

Artie grinned, gave a half-hearted wave back, and let his foot off the brake. Just before the car slipped into the garage next to Artie's gym he noticed something at the man's feet he hadn't noticed until that moment. It was an overflowing bucket of popcorn.

NINE

ARTIE RAN THE HURRICANE BRUSH across the tile in the room he referred to as the 'killing floor'. He'd managed to push most of the blood down the drain he'd installed in the center of the floor and had since scrubbed, polished, and buffed another five times each. The overkill was mainly due to Artie wanting to really put his As Seen On T.V. 3-in-1 Scrubber, Polisher, and Buffer System to the test.

It worked like a charm, just as Artie knew it would, but he purposely took his time so he could think. The strange man with super straight hair and a bucket of popcorn had spread a bad taste across the palate of Artie's mind. The killing of the young panhandler, while being a much needed stress reliever, hadn't settled him as much as he had hoped.

All he could think about was the dried drop of blood along with myriad other things revolving around his visit to Bloomwalls that morning and, now, the stranger next door. On top of that, ghostly remnants of the odd dream stuck to portions of his memory but were translucent and hard to read. These added stressors didn't allow him to fully enjoy the kill as much as he would under normal circumstances, but a kill was a kill and he didn't take it for granted.

Finally satisfied with the cleanliness of his 'killing floor' room, Artie turned out the light and turned on the industrial exhaust fan in the ceiling before he closed the door. Artie had a stack of new As Seen On T.V. products waiting for him to peruse, examine, and discover the many uses of, but as much as he wanted to revel in the intoxicating effect this would have on him, he couldn't let himself yet. He had to either figure out where the drop of blood in the living room came from or convince himself he knew where it came from before he allowed himself any other form of relaxation.

Artie had put off further investigation of the spot by prolonging his cleaning because it presented the possibility he was not as in control of things as he obsessively needed to be. The thought terrified Artie in a way he hadn't experienced since he first started killing.

Artie had almost all but forgotten how it felt; fear had crept back and perched in the familiar part of Artie's mind he'd evicted it from years ago. He walked on shaky legs down the hall as he left the 'killing floor' on his way to the living room. He honestly wasn't sure what he would gain from looking at the spot again, and fear worked at twisting his guts a bit tighter with each step he took.

Artie stood in the hall for a few seconds before entering the living room to stay himself and push out the fear. From where he stood, the light reflecting off the high-gloss finish of the wood floor hid the spot. He slowly approached from the hall and kept his eyes glued to where he knew the spot to be, but the reflected light changed the closer he got, like it was purposely concealing it from him.

Artie stepped in front of where the dime-size blood drop was and blocked the light with his body. He got down on his hands and knees and put his face to the floor so his cheek was almost touching it as he examined the area up close. He pulled his head back up and slowly scanned back and forth several more times.

The fear twisting his guts morphed to confusion, and by the time he stood, it exploded into full-blown rage. The spot of dried blood was gone.

TEN

ARTIE WAS INTERESTED TO SEE how the Reverse Ionized Dust Eliminator he'd picked up that morning worked, and while he currently didn't have a deck attached to his house, he wanted to figure out a way to test the All in One Deck Sander and Sealer he'd gotten as well. He didn't do either though, and the new line of As Seen On T.V. items he'd bought hours earlier remained stacked neatly by the front door, unopened.

As much as he wanted to play with his new toys he simply couldn't wrangle together enough focus to do so. Artie had pulled a chair up to where the spot had been, but he hadn't been able to sit down in it yet. He stared at the floor as if he were expecting the spot to appear before his eyes like it had only gone into hiding temporarily. This wasn't the case, of course, and Artie knew it but still couldn't stop staring.

He posed the question to himself of how likely it was he'd imagined the spot a dozen times over, but he just couldn't convince himself he had. Artie considered the fact his dream had caused mild disorientation when he'd first woken up, but was it that disorienting? Hadn't he been late to Bloomwalls because he'd been examining the spot for so long? He decided there were only two options as to what happened.

Either he had imagined the spot or it had been there and was then cleaned up sometime between when he left and when he'd finished with the panhandler. The problem was he couldn't prove either, knowing it was damn near impossible to get into his house due to the array of locks on every possible entrance and a security system he'd modeled with surprises of his own. Artie didn't believe someone came in and cleaned without him knowing. On the other hand, he couldn't and wouldn't believe the possibility of his mind deceiving him in such a way.

He'd been vacillating on the stalemate he'd reached with himself and decided he couldn't think about it anymore; at least not for a while. Artie decided to confront the other issue bothering him, which was the presence of the strange man next door and his odd, mismatched appearance. Who was he, and why did he wave so emphatically at Artie? He was going to walk across to Ms. Lancaster's house and ask her about the man staying in her garage. Artie stood up and headed for the front door, running his fingers along the top of the stack of As Seen On T.V. items before walking outside. He'd be back to tend to them soon, but he just needed to find out the answer to at least one of the questions he had that day.

He strolled across his front yard to Ms. Lancaster's door, not wanting to rush or seem eager despite currently being a walking bag of anxiety. He stepped up onto the stoop, and just as he pulled his arm back to knock, he heard something and stopped. It was a familiar sound, but he wasn't sure where he knew it from? The sound came again before he had time to look in the right direction, and Artie spun in a full circle before finding the sound's origin.

Standing in front of Ms. Lancaster's garage was the man who'd been watering the plants when Artie pulled up. His ultra-straight hair had taken on a bit of a shine like it was wet, and the ends had started to curl up slightly. Artie made eye-contact with the man just in time to see his doughy, wet lips twitch as he spat a peculiar sound from the back of his throat.

ELEVEN

ARTIE STOOD IN FRONT OF Ms. Lancaster's garage apartment, pacing, trying to decide if he was crazy or not. There were too many things about the day that left him unsettled and slightly shaken, although you'd never tell by looking at him. The goofy, outgoing veneer he coated himself with was thick and sturdy from the years of heavy application and from practicing dissociation.

Artie had conditioned himself to always appear happy or aloof or both. Anyone who happened to walk by would see him smiling admiringly at the various potted plants arranged in front of his neighbor's garage. Perhaps he was helping with the plant's care and cultivation, or maybe he viewed them with a tinge of playful jealousy over his neighbor's green thumb?

Artie looked on and smiled, but beneath the surface he seethed with rage that ran hot through his veins. Artie had made the mistake of momentarily looking away from the man who made the sound and back to the door he was about to knock on. He couldn't have taken his eyes off him for more than half a second, but in that brief moment, he heard a door slam. When Artie looked back, the man was gone.

He decided against knocking on Ms. Lancaster's door to ask about her odd boarder, not wanting to get the woman involved. If something was wrong with Artie, if he'd blown a gasket and was slowly losing his mind, he didn't want to bring his psychosis to anyone's attention.

Instead, he casually strolled up the driveway to have a look around the garage turned apartment. Originally the structure had been a regular, detached, two-car garage until the Lancasters added a second-story room to it for their teenage son. When he moved out and went to college, the retired Mr. Lancaster decided he needed a project to work on, so he set to converting the first floor of the garage as well.

Artie remembered coming home, sometimes as late as two or so in the morning, with his next kill in the trunk and finding Mr. Lancaster still working away or even sometimes taking a break to smoke a cigarette in the driveway. Artie would wave, Mr. Lancaster would wave back, and there would be no other mention of it. He liked that about Mr. Lancaster. If something didn't directly involve him he could give a shit less, which was a great quality in a neighbor.

When he was finished, Mr. Lancaster had turned the garage into what basically equated to a two-story townhouse. Artie marveled at Lancaster's craftsmanship and how you truly could not tell the space had ever been used to house cars and store lawn equipment. It was immaculate and beautiful.

When Artie asked what Mr. Lancaster planned on doing with the place, he joked about using it himself when he was in the 'dog house' with the wife. He never had a chance to use the place as an escape from martial woes because two days later Mr. Lancaster had a massive stroke and died. He had been in the driveway smoking a cigarette when it happened, and Artie was the one who found him when he returned from a morning voyage to Bloomwalls.

Artie leapt from his car to render aid but could tell the man was already dead by the time he was within five feet of him. He found it sad and ironic that he knelt by the man and began giving him chest compressions in an attempt to revive him when he was typically engaged in doing the opposite.

After that, Ms. Lancaster would occasionally rent the space out for short periods of time with most of her boarders being transplants who needed a temporary place while they looked for a permanent one. Artie hadn't interacted with any of the boarders past a nod and a smile and only if they happened to be outside while he was coming or going. None of them ever tried to interact with Artie further until now.

Artie continued to pace while racking his brain for a memory of this man from his past. He'd moved around a lot, so it wasn't outside the realm of possibility this person was an acquaintance from another town Artie had forgotten. He wondered if this was a sign he needed to pull up stakes again and start over somewhere else? Artie was comfortable here though and had managed to remain fairly inconspicuous, so moving was something he wanted to avoid if possible.

Barring he hadn't lost it and this man was real and not some projection of his psychosis, Artie would get to the bottom of it. He wanted to casually introduce himself to the man and see if perhaps an up-close, face-to-face meeting would jog his memory. If not, Artie would just ask point blank if he knew the man from somewhere and feign recognition when he was told.

The only thing keeping Artie from having already knocked on the door was the fear of finding the man wasn't real. If he imagined the blood, and he imagined the man, and he imagined the sound, it meant there was something very wrong with Artie.

Like tearing off a bandage, he stepped up to the door and knocked loudly three times. His heart was pounding, but he kept his breathing slow and steady. Artie clenched his teeth and knocked three more times just as hard. He tilted his ear to the door, straining to hear anything to indicate someone was inside, but all he heard was a muted *ping* sound in sporadic succession. He was about to administer a third pounding to the door, but as he brought his arm back he looked down and saw something. Three kernels of popcorn blew gently across the toes of his shoes like tiny, white tumbleweeds.

TWELVE

ARTIE DIDN'T FALL INTO HIS usual lengthy, post-kill sleep after having dispatched the panhandler. For the past four and a half hours he'd been sitting in his house in the dark, looking out the window in his bedroom that gave him a clear view of the front of Ms. Lancaster's garage apartment.

The new As Seen On T.V. products he'd been very much looking forward to learning about and experimenting with remained stacked just inside the front door where they'd been for hours. It wasn't often something came up in Artie's life that took precedent over the obsession he felt partially defined by, but this was a wholly unique situation. The popcorn kernels he saw outside the apartment door just before he was about to beat it down proved to Artie he wasn't crazy.

He knew he saw a bucket of popcorn at the man's feet when he pulled into his own garage just before noon. Artie hadn't officially seen the man go inside, but after the door slammed, the pudgy, little weirdo was nowhere to be seen, so it stood to reason he'd gone inside.

Artie had been sure of it at the time, but his certainty dwindled as hours passed without a sign of anyone leaving the apartment. If the man was inside, as Artie suspected, it meant he'd ignored the knocking on his door. Artie considered ignoring someone to be very rude, and the thought burned him up on the inside like his blood had turned to mercury by way of alchemy gone wrong. Under normal circumstances he would let himself into the man's apartment and show him just how rude he thought it was, but this was a different case.

This man was the missing piece of a puzzle Artie had been trying to put together since he started hearing the sound in his dreams. Artie very badly wanted to kill this troll of a man and he would, too, but not until the puzzle was complete. He'd learned to be patient and could stay his urge until the time was right.

The longer he waited, the more he thought about the events of the day and what this man's involvement may have been. The significance of the portly boarder's straight, grease-free hair and the bucket of popcorn at his feet hadn't escaped Artie's attention. It was no coincidence the one new As Seen On T.V. item that was sold out, the one Artie needed to complete his collection of the new line, claimed to provide all three of those things.

The mystery man was one step ahead of Artie and had been so for who knew how long? He steadied himself against the unsettling thought. He'd always seen himself as stealthy and elusive in his acquisition of victims, but the thought he could have been secretly stalked the whole time made his accomplishment feel hollow and worthless.

Artie hadn't been in the living room since coming back inside. He didn't want to look at where the spot of blood had been again, mostly because he was afraid it would somehow have reappeared. He couldn't handle what that discovery would do to his brain, at least not now. He knew what he saw that morning and what he didn't see that afternoon, and he was certain it had something to do with the mystery boarder next door.

Just as dusk was busy lightly dusting the daytime sky, Artie saw the doorknob begin to turn. He sat straight up, fully alert and focused, having ripped the daydreams away like cobwebs from a corner. The door slowly opened, and the man stepped out with his back to Artie. He shut the door and turned a key to engage the lock before turning around.

The man's appearance had changed to the extent Artie didn't think it was the same person, but only for a moment. That was all it took to realize it was indeed the same guy and Artie keyed in on what was different about him now. The man's hair was no longer aggressively straight, having instead reverted to its natural state, which was a mop of dark curls so greasy they reflected what little light was left into Artie's eyes from across the driveway.

The man looked around like he was expecting someone, and then leveled his gaze across the driveway through the window Artie sat behind. When the man's eyes met his, Artie remembered.

Every detail about the dream he'd had the night prior flooded his consciousness as if the strange man's eyes had broken the dam holding them back. He remembered the odd looking, lumpy, acne-faced man from his dream and how he'd been looking through the window. Artie remembered throwing the coffee mug at the man's head and how he jumped through the window and slid across the floor.

Artie saw himself in his mind smashing the man's face into the hardwood repeatedly, and he remembered the blood. Blood he'd found a drop of in the same spot on the living room floor. Fear gripped his heart with a cold, skeletal hand, reminding him again it was back, and he leapt from his chair.

Artie was afraid what had happened between the short, round man and him was not a dream. He went through all the details again, trying to find something that stuck out to make him know it couldn't have really happened, but it wasn't that easy. There were too many questions he didn't know the answer to, but he knew who did. Artie left the window and walked out the front door to confront the man and fill in the blanks.

THIRTEEN

ARTIE STOOD OVER THE PILED-UP boxes of the new As Seen On T.V. products he'd purchased fifteen hours earlier. They were still next to the front door. Only now he couldn't decide whether to begin the process of opening them one by one, slowly taking in all each product had to offer, or kick the pile over and stomp the contents of each box to tiny bits of plastic.

He'd missed him. He didn't know how it was possible, but the greasy-headed prick was gone by the time Artie had rushed out the front door. All he saw was a pair of taillights attached to an orange Fiero disappear up the street and around the corner. Artie noticed the unfamiliar car parked there earlier in the day but had since been too distracted to give it much thought.

Artie wondered if he'd reacted as quickly as he thought. The rush of recognizing the man and remembering his dream all at once could've momentarily skewed his perception of time. Still, the idea he'd moved slow enough for the man's chubby stump-legs to get him down the driveway and into his car fast enough to drive away before Artie could get outside seemed unreasonable.

He contemplated jumping in his Tempo and chasing after the man, but decided against it. Things could get ugly in a public setting where Artie would have little to no control, potentially bringing heat his way. He'd flown under the radar for the last twenty-two years, and he was going to stay that way. Artie knew the man existed, knew the significance he had to the dream *and* the goddamned sound, and sooner or later the piece of shit Fiero would be back on the curb.

Artie would handle this his way. He'd get his answers. Artie decided to go with neither plan for the stack of boxes, still not feeling up to engaging himself with them in any way. Instead he slunk to the kitchen, the soles of his shoes squeaking with each step across the clean, polished wood. He left the light off, still not wanting to see if the blood spot had reappeared.

He stepped in the kitchen and flipped on the lights that shown soft and white from beneath the cabinets. He opened the refrigerator and pulled out a bottle of beer he'd made himself with his As Seen On T.V. Home-Brew in Half the Time Beer Machine and Bathtub Wine Fermenter. The beer he made tasted more like wine with an overall, dominating flavor of dishwater. That is, if eleven people had thrown up in the dishwater, one of them drank some of it, and threw up again.

Also, it had the consistency of chilled diarrhea, but Artie needed the alcohol to calm down so he twisted off the cap, tilted his head back, and chugged. He stepped back from the fridge and let the door close as he drank. He lowered the bottle, swallowed, and gagged against the uniquely awful taste.

He turned his head, fighting down a dry heave, and accidentally got a view of the living room floor through the cut-out in the wall from the kitchen. It was framed in a rectangle of dim light, but it stuck out to Artie as if he were seeing it under the sun during the brightest part of the day.

He didn't see the spot of blood. Just past where the spot had been was a small, semi-circle indentation in the wall. White specs of dust lay on the floor beneath the dent like the aftermath of a cocaine party. Artie started to lose focus in the corners of his eyes, and his head pounded from extreme inner pressure. Then, he threw up all over the front of the refrigerator and the floor all around him.

The beer tasted better coming back up.

FOURTEEN

ARTIE WASN'T CRAZY. HE WAS either being fucked with or he was dead. Someone, more than likely the fat man next door, was pulling some elaborate prank designed to break Artie. For what purpose, he had no idea, but maybe the family member of a victim found out who Artie was, tracked him down, and was toying with him before bringing down the hammer.

He'd thought about this happening and what he would do if it did. Not because he doubted his ability, but because Artie thought constantly about scenarios he had the potential to be in and how he would react. It was best practices like this that kept him from being caught, but these were learned practices. Artie could remember being sloppy in the beginning, rushing everything, forgetting to take his time, making an unnecessarily large mess.

As he grew more proficient in his craft he doubled back to some of his early work and took care of who he thought had the potential to be a loose end. He was confident, but Artie wouldn't succumb to hubris. As far-fetched as this theory sounded, it did possess a sliver of a percentage of a chance of happening.

There was a much higher probability Artie was dead, but even so he refused to accept that. Not because he was afraid of being dead, but because it was too easy, too 'Occam's Razor'. There were too many moving parts for this to be some creepy death-loop Artie would run through over and over for eternity. Not that he didn't recognize a death-loop would involve an equal amount of moving parts, if not more, but this felt different.

Whatever was happening, Artie knew it wasn't going to be something as easy to explain as 'being dead'. This felt far more sinister, personal, even intimate on a certain level. And that fat, greasy-headed fuck next door knew all about it. Whether it was a high-priced hoax or a drugged out death-trip, the whole thing was a twist in Artie's sack he aimed to get ironed out in a hurry.

When he had pulled himself together after vomiting across a third of his otherwise immaculate kitchen, he had no choice but to take a closer look at the wall, which meant he was going to have to observe the area where the blood spot had been. He turned on all the lights making the living room bright enough to perform surgery, which wasn't a coincidence.

In the light, Artie could see it all. The path across the room he'd thought was light coming through the window was now revealed to be stained and damaged from the man's secretion. The parts of the floor he slid across had gone pale yellow, and the gloss had been eaten away.

When Artie turned toward the indentation in the wall it was indeed there, and five or six inches in front of it was the spot of blood.

"I don't think I was dreaming any of this," Artie said out loud to himself.

It was comforting to hear a voice after hours of silence even if it was his own. Artie took a step toward the wall and heard the squeal of the Fiero's tires as they ground against the curb in front of Ms. Lancaster's house.

Artie turned on the ball of his foot to change direction and head for the front door. From outside, he heard the Fiero's door slam, followed by the awful three-in-one, wet, sucking sound he thought had been plaguing him from his imagination. Then, the lights went out in Artie's house and across the entire neighborhood.

FIFTEEN

WIND WHIPPED THE TREES IN Artie's yard like they were paper stage props as it howled up the street to announce the incoming storm. Artie saw lightning off in the distance when he had been sitting at the window earlier, but it hardly registered with him. Now the storm had closed the gap and was making its entrance in grand form.

Artie felt the first telltale drops of on oncoming downpour when he stepped outside and scanned the darkness, looking for any sign of the man. He looked down the driveway toward the entrance of the garage apartment, but the only stirring he saw was caused by the wind. Artie looked from the car in the street to the garage and back again but still saw no sign of the short, fat man. Then, between gusts of wind, he heard something rustle from the front of Ms. Lancaster's house.

Artie took a few steps away from his door to get a better look across the yard and was pelted by the fat, sloppy, drops of water falling fast from the sky. Through the darkness, Artie could see the man bent over in the small flowerbed that ran along the front of Ms. Lancaster's house. He could only see the lumpy lower half of his nemesis from where he stood, and the man appeared to be struggling with something on the ground among the prize-winning tulips.

Artie made a move but stopped himself and stepped back through the door into the entryway to retrieve an aluminum bat from the corner behind the stack of unopened As Seen On T.V. items. He moved silently across his lawn, picking up speed as he crossed the driveway into Ms.

Lancaster's yard.

When he was within feet of the man, Artie held the bat over his head with one hand and reached out with the other. He grabbed the still stooping man on the shoulder, spun him around, and brought the meaty part of the bat down hard against the side of his head. The man emitted a high-pitched whimper as he crumpled into himself and collapsed into the flowers.

Artie stood back horrified when he looked down and saw Ms. Lancaster lying before him, clutching a garden gnome she had been trying to bring in before the storm hit. Blood gushed from the wound on her head and soaked into the soil. Artie saw a flash of recognition followed by confusion in the woman's eyes just before she fell unconscious. A door slammed somewhere behind him. Artie had missed his man again.

SIXTEEN

Ms. LANCASTER LAY ON A stainless steel gurney in the middle of Artie's 'killing floor' room. She was still unconscious but wouldn't remain so for much longer, leaving Artie no other choice in how to handle the matter. He'd swung the bat too hard, making the mistake of letting his emotions get the better of him in the moment, and he knew it.

Even if it had been his intended target he'd hit, the blow could have had the undesired effect of incapacitating the man to the point of being useless to Artie. As upset as it made him that he'd accidentally attacked his neighbor, Artie looked at it as a positive. He'd gotten the ramped-up anxiety out of his system upon striking Ms. Lancaster, and now he could think clearly.

The electricity was still out, so there were no lights coming from the windows of the garage apartment to let Artie know the man was inside, but he knew he was in there; he'd heard the door slam.

Artie leaned on the handle of his As Seen On T.V. Quad-Pad Turbo Dust and Odor Eliminating Mop and stared at the rise and fall of his neighbor's chest. Killing her meant he would have to disappear again and reinvent himself in a town on the other side of the country. He was annoyed by this but knew he'd have to leave anyway, after he'd gotten what he wanted out of the man. There would be too much risk in staying where he was any longer.

He'd have to find a new house, a new Bloomwalls, even a new Donna, but those were the least of Artie's concerns right now. He liked

Ms. Lancaster and knew she didn't deserve this, but when it came to self-preservation Artie took no chances. He saw the woman's breathing turn to short, quick gasps, and she moaned as consciousness began to slowly beckon her awake.

With a smooth, mechanical motion, Artie stepped forward and slit Ms. Lancaster's throat with a razorblade he'd had wedged between his fingers. The grace and precision of his movement continued as he stepped back and away before being touched by a single drop from the aortal eruption. The shock and adrenaline woke Ms. Lancaster, and she struggled to cry out but her voice box had been taken out of commission. Artie turned around and faced the wall as Ms. Lancaster sputtered and gurgled through her final moments of life. He took no pleasure in this kill. Ms. Lancaster had been a good neighbor, and he'd liked her as well as Mr. Lancaster when he was alive.

Another thing that robbed Artie of the enjoyment he usually experienced was the kill was not on his terms. He was made to kill Ms. Lancaster because of the pestering blob-man. Artie recognized he was the one who mistook his neighbor for her portly renter, but he never would have made the mistake if the man had not put him into this situation. He had taken away the control and, that, Artie could not abide.

The last of Ms. Lancaster's life left her in one long, low, wet wheeze that escaped from her lungs through the slit in her throat. Artie's usual routine was to discard the body and clean directly after he was finished but, so much of his routine had already been broken, what was one more thing? He slipped into the hall through the partially open door of the 'killing floor' and closed it slowly without looking behind him.

He would be back to take care of Ms. Lancaster later, after he'd taken care of the fat, pock-faced piece of shit. Artie engaged all the locks on the door just in case anything else got beyond his control that evening. He didn't want to think it could be possible, but despite being confident, he was also realistic.

He'd already started formulating a plan but only had the basic skeleton so far. He went to the living room to think and watch for any sign of activity from the garage apartment. The living room was extra dark and quiet. Without electricity there was nothing running in the background to create the white noise he'd gotten used to ignoring.

The blood on the floor was gone and the dust from the damaged sheetrock was also absent, but this time it was because Artie cleaned them. There was no reason to attempt repairing the wall since he'd be leaving this house soon anyway. He paced the room, keeping his eyes on the window while building meat around the bones of his plan.

The second half of the plot was easy since it involved Artie employing various methods of torture, both learned and invented, on the man before ending his life. He didn't particularly like to torture people, but on the rare occasion he deemed one of his victims deserving of such brutality, he reveled in it. This would be one of those occasions.

Artie familiarized himself with methods of torture despite not being completely into it because he liked to be well-rounded and prepared. He'd used this research to invent torture tactics of his own and had even modified several As Seen On T.V. products to act as such. Artie tweaked a Wax-Vac, originally designed to suck wax from your ear, by adding a retractable screw and increasing the suction power by double digits.

When inserted into someone's ear, the suction would rupture the eardrum while the screw would poke and scramble the rest of the inner ear before sucking what was left out. Artie would then play on his victim's inability to hear as well as their equilibrium being turned to garbage. He would poke and prod at them from behind, and even better, Artie would open the shackles or untie the rope he was using to detain the person. When the victim stood up and took a step, thinking they had a chance to escape, they would tip over and crumple to the ground, their sense of balance long gone.

The modified Wax-Vac might be a good place to start, but Artie wondered if it was too good for the man across the driveway. The wind picked up and flung fat raindrops, popping like overripe berries against the window. His view of the garage was blurred, but he could still see well enough to know if something changed.

The intensity of the rain reminded Artie of another favorite torture tactic involving an older model Hurricane Scrub Brush. He modified it so high-pressure hot water shot from the tiny nozzles designed to feed soap into the brush, but he'd removed the bristles. He would place it on a part of the victim, like their stomach, and press the trigger on the handle to release the water in short spurts.

It was the equivalent of being jabbed over and over with tiny, burning hot needles, causing a ton of excruciating pain. Later they'd have a hole in their stomach and a slow death ahead. Artie thought something like this might be better suited for the man in question, only he would make sure to take his sweet time, as he would with most things he planned to do to the man.

Artie could pace for hours thinking of torture tactics, but none of it meant anything if he couldn't get the pudgy nuisance into his house. He could always improvise if the situation called for it. If Artie broke into the garage apartment and was put into a position where he would have to kill the man there, then so be it.

Artie realized, however, if he were forced to kill the fat nuisance inside the garage apartment it would be another way for control to be taken away. The man would be dead and still hold that power over Artie. He promised himself he'd get the greasy, crater-faced fool back to the house and use the 'killing floor' to the fullest extent before shutting it down, at least for now.

He thought about Ms. Lancaster lying strapped to a gurney in that same room and felt a tinge of sadness over the senselessness of her death. She would be pretty well bled out by now, with most of the mess having worked its way down the floor drain. Artie would have to work around her once he got the man in the room but planned on disposing of her as respectfully as possible before leaving the house for good.

Artie became momentarily lost in swirling thoughts of torturous revenge when he heard glass shatter and snapped out of it. He ran over to the window and threw it open despite the rain so his view would not be obstructed. The window next to the front door of the garage apartment was broken, popcorn pouring out in large amounts.

The tightly packed kernels pressed against each other to form one giant mass of popcorn. The way it forced itself through the broken window reminded him of one of the fireworks he played with as a kid. It was a small, black disc you placed on the ground, and when you touched a flame to it the thing would start to grow, making it look like a snake was crawling out of the ground. What he was looking at now was like that but on a completely different level.

The popcorn didn't last long in the rain and quickly melted into buttery, white mush that pooled around the driveway like watery, pissed on snow. The popcorn snake continued to push its way through the window with no sign of stopping, and to Artie, appeared to be gaining momentum.

Within seconds, the space between Artie's window and the garage apartment was covered with buttered kernels in various stages of decay as the rain drove down harder. Through the pounding rain, wailing wind, and thunderclaps, Artie swore he heard laughter.

SEVENTEEN

ARTIE BROKE FROM THE OPEN window to head for the front door but stopped short after a step. He'd already been burned in his pursuit and knew he didn't have the extra three seconds to exit his home properly. He didn't want to risk going out the front door to find a completely different scene than the one he was currently seeing.

He turned, stepped back up to the window, grabbed the sill, and leapt through. The popcorn snowbank had closed the distance between the apartment and the side of Artie's house, and he slipped in the slop, landing hard on his chest. The popcorn completely covered him as he lay there gasping, but Artie forced himself to his feet to keep his eye on the apartment. The popcorn was up to his knees, and the wetter it got, the harder it was for Artie to wade through. He choked down what few shallow breaths he could manage to suck in and battled against the rising slosh of snack food.

Artie was halfway across the driveway now, and the popcorn had risen to his waist with no signs of stopping. He heard the distinctive snap of wood splintering and looked up to see the door to the garage apartment bulging out as the frame buckled under the pressure building behind it. A second later, the door broke away with a crack loud enough to rival the booming thunder.

Popcorn filled the open doorway and flooded out, adding to the deluge that had taken over the driveway, and was now starting to spill out into the street. Before the fallen door could be completely covered by the approaching avalanche, Artie reached out and grabbed for it. He pulled himself forward through the rising wave of wet popcorn, using the small amount of leverage the door gave him.

Artie popped his head up and was able to see the splintered doorframe within reach, so he dove forward and reached all around him until his hands landed on the solid wood. He didn't know what he was going to do once he got inside the popcorn filled apartment, but he would figure it out.

Holding onto the doorframe, Artie pulled against the warm kernels rushing against him. When he'd managed to yank himself across the threshold, he began to fall through the popcorn, but when he got to where the floor should have been, he didn't stop falling. Artie spun and reached blindly around for something to grab onto but came away with handfuls of crushed kernels and buttery fingers. Artie's eyes were open, but all he could see was a blur of white until he suddenly landed hard on his back. Then the white faded into black.

EIGHTEEN

ARTIE'S EYES WERE OPEN BUT he couldn't see anything. He wasn't sure if it was truly that dark wherever he was or if he had actually gone blind. He moved his hands across the floor around him, hoping to find a clue as to where he was and how to get out. All he felt was cold concrete without a crack or divot to speak of. It made Artie think about his As Seen On T.V. Perfect Spread Cement Smoother with Built in Alarm Clock and how he hadn't had a chance to use it yet. He wondered if the product was, in fact, used on the very floor he lay on now.

It took Artie longer than it normally would to move his arms up and across his chest. He rubbed his forearms, expecting his hands to come back slick and greasy with artificial butter flavored popcorn topping oil, but his skin was dry and no slicker than usual. A soft whirring sound started up and seemed a ways off from where Artie lay on the cool, smooth concrete, but it was getting closer.

He allowed his head to roll to the left, which, as best he could tell, was the direction the sound was approaching from. Still unsure if he had gone blind or not, he couldn't tell if the two tiny green lights he saw were real or just his brain shooting fireworks across the insides of his useless eyes. He stared and blinked and stared some more until his eyes watered up, turning the lights to blurred, minty stars leaving streaks of tracers until he blinked them back into focus.

Now Artie knew he wasn't blind but was still unable to lift his limbs without exerting the maximum amount of effort. It was so dark it didn't matter if he was able to see or move since neither would do him any good within the complete darkness he'd been swallowed by. All Artie could do was watch the two tiny green stars approach him as the whirring sound grew louder the closer it got.

A spotlight shone down from somewhere above and sliced through the darkness with the precision an expert hand would guide a ginsu knife through a thick pork shank. Artie only glimpsed the light at first, since the sudden luminous change shocked his eyes into actual blindness until they were able to adjust. When his vision returned, he saw the spotlight shining down from an impossibly high ceiling, far too high for Artie to see where it originated.

He followed the light back down to the floor to see the short, fat, greasy man illuminated as he worked the As Seen On T.V. Perfect Spread Cement Smoother with Built in Alarm Clock back and forth across the already ultra-smooth cement. The two green lights Artie had seen were on the front of the machine the man was guiding. It looked like a slightly modified version of an industrial floor buffer, and Artie wondered if the man had unlocked the full potential of the item the designers had locked away within the cold, plastic-metal outer casing just as he himself had done with the majority of his As Seen On T.V. products.

The man stopped advancing when he got within twenty feet and worked the machine across the section of floor in front of him. Sweat dripped from the short, fat man's forehead in comically large, viscous drops like what would be in a cat and mouse cartoon. He didn't look up, but instead stayed intensely engaged in the work he was doing. Artie almost called out but thought better of it, wanting to make sure he was able to move at least somewhat before engaging the sweaty madman.

Artie lifted his arms off his chest with slightly more ease than he had putting them there. Gravity helped, of course, and his arms fell heavily back to the concrete floor with a slap, audible to Artie, but not loud enough for the man to hear over the machine. Artie sat still another moment, waiting for some kind of response, but the man didn't so much as glance in his direction. The man continued to sweat and smooth the already extra smooth floor in front of him.

Artie attempted to bend his knees and push himself up into a sitting position, but a pain shot up from the base of his spine, ceasing his movement and causing his limbs to again lie flat against the floor. He was worried he'd permanently damaged his spinal cord, and while he could sort of move, there was still the debilitating effect it would have on him in the long run. How would he do his work? How would he get to Bloomwalls for all his As Seen On T.V. needs?

The whirring from the machine stopped suddenly, and Artie glanced over to see his nemesis staring directly at him. The man's mouth pursed and spit the sound across the room, where it bounced and echoed off the floor and unseen walls and ceiling.

"What is this?" Artie finally managed. "What do you want, you fat piece of shit?"

The man's shiny, thick lips twitched, making the sound again, while Artie cringed against its slow decay in the large, empty room. Instead of responding, the man smiled and turned the machine back on. A moment later, the green lights on the front turned red and flashed in time to an obnoxious bleating emanating from the inner workings of the contraption. It was the built-in alarm clock feature.

Hearing it gave Artie some small glimpse of hope he was perhaps dreaming this whole horrible situation and was about to wake up in his own bed with a full range of motion. The alarm continued on obnoxiously while Artie willed himself to wake from a dream he wasn't really having.

"Well, fuck you anyway, you slimy freak!" Artie screamed across the distance between them. "You better hope I'm paralyzed because if not things are gonna get real ugly for you."

The man still didn't speak, but flashed a wide smile, opening his mouth to reveal his crooked yellow teeth had been replaced by several rows of sharp teeth filling his maw with deadly, razor-like stalactites and stalagmites. The alarm sound continued, bouncing around the cavernous space, getting louder and louder. Saliva dripped and hung from the bottom of his chin in thick strands of mucus that fell slowly, like a slow-motion bungee jump gone wrong.

Artie blinked and the man was suddenly upon him. His hands had been replaced with thick, sharp talons he used to rip into Artie's chest while straddling his supine form. Heat flooded Artie's body as what felt like knives of fire dug into his stomach, destroying organs while cooking him from the inside out. He certainly couldn't move now, and screaming was out of the question, since his lungs had not only been punctured, but completely shredded.

The man-turned-beast stopped tearing into his torso and leaned in close to Artie's ear, making the dreaded sound again, but this time at earsplitting volume. He lifted his head and bared his fangs one more time before plunging back down to rip a huge chunk out of Artie's neck. The heat in his body turned to ice, and he felt himself slip away as his body was devoured.

NINETEEN

ARTIE OPENED HIS EYES TO a bright, white light, and they burned as a warm, slimy substance leaked into them. He brought his hands to his eyes and began to rub, realizing suddenly he not only wasn't paralyzed and in pieces, but he wasn't in the dark room anymore.

He quickly discovered rubbing his eyes was no help and was, in fact, aiding in allowing more of the slime to get beneath his lids. He took his hands from his face to find they were covered in grease, and when he tried to take a step, he knew exactly where he was. He was back in the popcorn-filled garage apartment and was able to confirm it when he managed to open his eyes the tiniest bit. As he regained focus, he saw the off-white, buttered up kernels he was completely buried in.

What just happened with Artie and the man on the dark, concrete floor must have really been a dream, but it didn't feel like it was? Artie could still feel phantom pain in his neck and heat pulsing through his system from down in his guts. He thought he was fed up and angry before, but now those emotions had been accelerated to the nth degree. The thought of destroying the mystery fat man consumed Artie's mind as he pushed against the popcorn barrier in front of him, crushing kernels against his slick, buttered up body.

The muffled snap and crackle of the kernels as he crushed through them became progressively louder the farther he went until it reached a deafening peak, but Artie was still able to hear something else through the din. He paused, silencing the crunching of his advancement to listen, and while the sound was very familiar, he was baffled as to why he couldn't place it. Then, it hit him. Popcorn. It was the sound of popcorn popping somewhere just beyond the popcorn sea he was swimming through.

Artie plowed forward with renewed vigor, knowing if he didn't get to the popping and stop it, the popcorn would become more and more dense, further impeding his progress. Worse than that, if the popcorn didn't stop popping it would not only keep him from advancing, but the ever-increasing volume would push back and force Artie out the way he came in. He didn't think it was possible for popcorn to pack together tightly enough to crush him beneath it, but it very well could asphyxiate him if he wasn't careful.

The popping sound began to suddenly increase, not in volume but speed and frequency. Artie's fear began to materialize as the spaces between pops became non-existent and the wall of popcorn's yield against his pushing lessened significantly. He was wrong about not being able to be crushed by popcorn as he now felt the increasing weight push down on him hard. He crouched as the fluffy, buttery cocoon thickened and stiffened around him as he racked his brain to come up with a quick plan. The cartoonish idea of eating his way out presented itself. Artie quickly dismissed this, realizing the fact he had this thought to begin with meant he was starting to panic.

Through the popping and the crunching, Artie heard the distinct wet, sucking characteristics of the familiar sound from the man's sopping lips. Hearing it triggered the release of hidden strength reserved for times of crisis such as the one Artie was experiencing at this moment. He shot forward from his crouched position; his legs launched him with the force of industrial, coiled springs, and Artie was surprised he was able to get enough purchase from a floor slick with imitation butter product.

His body shot through the popcorn barrier like a missile launched from a submarine. When he felt his momentum begin to wane, Artie used his arms, attempting a bastardized breaststroke to aid his propulsion. The popcorn became impossibly thick the farther he got, and he began to furiously move his legs and arms like he was swimming for his life while a great white nipped at his heels.

Artie closed his eyes against the stinging salt and butter-stuff and put his arms out for another stroke only to discover he could feel open air between his fingers. He struggled to get his hands all the way through, then used them to grab hold of the sides of the small hole he'd created in order to gain the leverage needed to pull himself out.

When he pushed his head through the opening, Artie gasped, taking in a lungful of fresh air followed by a coughing fit resulting in several errant kernels being forced from his throat. He had been so focused on getting out he didn't even realize the popcorn had already been working at asphyxiating him. Once his head was free, he was able to worm the rest of the way through the delicious, makeshift birth canal and smacked down hard against what felt like cool, kitchen linoleum.

His vision was a blur from the popcorn residue, and Artie did his best to blink his eyes back into focus, knowing rubbing them with greasy fingers wasn't going to help. He looked up and around, each blink bringing the room more into focus until he could see enough to make it out. He was right about being in the kitchen, and sitting at the table, looking down at him, was the man. Strewn across the kitchen table were five As Seen On T.V. Greaseless Hair De-Greaser, Straightener, and Popcorn Makers.

Also on the table in front of the man was a yellow, plastic bowl of popcorn. Strangely enough, the rest of the kitchen was popcorn-free, aside from the few kernels that had been stuck to Artie when he pulled himself out and were now scattered on the floor around him. The man took a single kernel from the bowl, placed it in his mouth, and chewed slowly before turning his attention back to Artie.

"Well," he said, eyebrows raised. "You ready to talk yet?"

TWENTY

ARTIE WASN'T A KILLER BY choice, but he chose to not get caught. From the beginning, he'd taken the care other killers, even the more prevalent ones with long careers, either never thought to do or simply couldn't pull off. Either that or they got lazy, wanted to quit, or just wanted to get caught because there was nothing else left for them to do. He wasn't perfect though, and, of course, Artie had made some mistakes along the way but nothing that ended up being of detriment to him.

Even with the few close calls he'd had early on, Artie managed to skate by unscathed without appearing on any law enforcement radar. He prided himself on having never left any of his DNA with or around his victims, but this was mostly due to Artie bringing victims back to his place of residence to do what he referred to as 'disposing of properly'.

Artie had never been arrested nor had he ever even gotten a traffic ticket, so there was no trace of him in any database. He'd never had to submit fingerprints or have his mouth swabbed, and, as far as Artie knew, he'd not once even been a suspect or person of interest in any of the murders he'd committed. For a man with a hundred plus kills under his belt, Artie had kept his nose incredibly clean.

He didn't consider himself lucky per se, but then again Artie never believed in luck or gave much thought to how he'd gone so long without the slightest blemish on his record. He truly believed it was solely his careful planning and expertise that kept him forever one step ahead of

Johnny Law. He'd never once entertained the thought of there being any reason other than his own expertise keeping him from being caught.

Artie had not considered the possibility of someone or something intervening on his behalf in some way because there was no reason to. He had no friends and never became anything more than an acquaintance to anyone in whatever town he happened to inhabit at any given time. Even with his current, now both late, neighbors, he kept his distance, allowing for only short, surface interactions with him. Other than that, Artie interacted with Donna at Bloomwalls more than anyone else in town, and he was in no danger of her being able to pick him out of a lineup.

These were the thoughts running through Artie's head as he looked up from the floor to the fat, greasy butterball sitting at the table eating popcorn.

"Talk?" Artie coughed the word more than spoke it and spit out several more whole kernels from the back of his throat. "Talk about what? Who . . . who the hell are you anyway? What the hell is going on here?!?'

Artie made an attempt to stand while hurling angry questions, but the buttery grease coating every inch of his body did not allow him the grip needed to push himself up. His hands slid out to the sides in front of him, and his chin hit the linoleum hard enough to make him see stars, but he didn't dare let himself pass out.

Artie's entire body clenched against the electric pulse of pain in his jaw while the man remained at the table calmly eating popcorn one kernel at a time. He watched Artie slip and struggle a second and third time before finally being able to make it to his feet. The amount of effort Artie exerted left him rubber-armed and out of breath.

"Sit," said the man, gesturing to a chair opposite him at the table. His voice was deeper than Artie remembered it being.

"Answer me!" shouted Artie, unable to keep his voice from cracking as he shrieked.

The man brushed the salt sticking to his fingertips on a napkin he produced from his lap. He pushed his chair back from the table and turned in his seat to face Artie.

"You can call me . . . Art."

The man's words fell flat enough to eradicate all meaning, so it took Artie a second to process them.

"Art? Are you serious? That wouldn't happen to be short for Artie, would it?"

Artie's brain had finally fully reengaged since he'd nearly been smothered to death by an avalanche of popped corn, and he remembered what he was there to do.

"As a matter of fact, it is."

Artie's desire to kill the tiny, oil-slick of a man and shut off his smart-ass mouth forever overwhelmed him to the point of acting on it, but as quickly as it came on, it was gone. It was like he'd suddenly forgotten what he was in the middle of doing, and Artie strained to grasp at the ghost of a memory.

"All right, Artie," the man who called himself Art said, hopping down from the chair. "I'm going to do some talking now, and I'd like you to shut up and listen."

Three random kernels popped from one of the machines on the table, and Artie couldn't help but flinch. He regretted it immediately.

TWENTY-ONE

"**HAVE YOU EVER WONDERED WHY** you're the way you are? Why you do what you do?"

Artie gritted his teeth and held his tongue. He would give 'Art' a chance to speak for now, while he assessed the rest of the small kitchen looking for something he could use to his advantage when he deemed the time was right.

"It's because of me," continued Art. "Art is short for Artie because, while I'm technically not *you*, I am a part of you."

Artie couldn't help but roll his eyes.

"Oh, I know how it sounds," Art said, using the back of his hand to wipe drool from the corner of his fat, wet lips, smearing flakes of half-dry, white crust across his cheek, "but I am telling you the truth. I am the urge, the push, the whisper. I used to be why you killed, but I have since become what allows you to kill."

Artie's anger grew with each word spilling from the slimy lips of the bloated troll-man. No one and nothing *allowed* him to do anything. Artie was in complete and total control of what he did.

"I know you think you're the one who controls the impulses you have. You believe you pick the victims, and you divvy out suffering or lack thereof as you see fit, but I'm afraid that's just not true."

From what Artie could see, the only items worth using as a weapon were on the far side of the kitchen just beyond Art. A cast iron frying pan rested atop the stove, and a knife block on the counter was pushed back against the wall, hiding in the shadow of the cabinets hanging above. Artie was confident he could do the necessary damage with either item, but he still didn't trust his footing not to betray him if he made a quick move.

"Allow me to explain," began Art.

"Please do," Artie hissed through a tightly locked jaw.

Art paused and his fat slug-lips curled up slowly at the edges, causing more of the white crust collected there to flake and fall like sickening snowflakes.

"As I was saying," Art smacked his shiny lips, "allow me to explain. There is something inside of people like you, but not all people. I understand it's a commonly held belief all people have some kind of 'killer instinct' built into their DNA or psyche, but it has been suppressed by thousands of years of evolution and civility. This, I assure you, could not be further from the truth because, if it were, the human species as a whole would have wiped itself out some time ago."

Artie was half listening, still trying to devise the most effective move he could make that would result in the least resistance. Art wiped the back of his other hand across the oily beads of sweat on his forehead, popping several zits in the process.

For the second time, Artie heard the distinct snap of skin stretched tight with irritation over small white protrusions rupture against the pressure applied. Under different circumstances, Artie would be disgusted by the thin streams of blood-diluted pus slowly leaking from pinhole wounds down Art's forehead, but now he remained unfazed.

"What makes people kill, what *allows* them to perform an act deemed most heinous is not something lying dormant in people, waiting for the right situation to awaken the sinister urge and turn them into a killing machine. It's actua—"

"It's actually you," interrupted Artie. "Is that what you're trying to tell me, huh? The only reason people kill is because *you* are allowing them too?"

Art's purplish, scabby jelly-lips twitched and pursed, and Artie flinched involuntarily as his brain anticipated a sound that didn't come. He looked from Art's lips up to his eyes in time to see the last hint of frustration fade away. Artie assessed Art was probably using a method to curb his anger-based impulses, like counting to ten or one of the many others learned from a court-ordered anger management class. He was impressed by Art's display of discipline.

"No, Artie."

The words fell like dead baby birds from an abandoned nest, and Art paused, anticipating another interruption. When it didn't come, he continued.

"I'm not an omnipresent god of death. I am *your* urge to kill, and yours alone, just as all other killers have *their* own personal urge unique to them. Anytime a person kills another person, even if by complete accident, it's because they have an urge, and whether they're aware of it or not, the urge must be acted on or it will act out itself.

"In a lot of cases, mostly with accidental killings, the urge is satiated for good and remains dormant. In other cases, such as yours, the urge is not so easily satisfied and remains active for much longer. Some even for as long as the person is alive."

Artie felt his legs getting farther apart as his shoes slowly slid on a butter-flavored oil slick he didn't realize had slowly spread to catch up to where he stood. He glanced behind him at the wall of popcorn packed tight floor to ceiling, but it looked fake and eerie, like a set piece for a movie about a haunted concession stand or a popcorn house. Yellow-tinted grease leaked from beneath the wall and oozed, intent on covering the floor like a busted oil tanker trying to blacken the sea.

"The best way to describe the relationship between these specific people and their specific urge would be symbiotic, but even that's not entirely true," Art continued. "The two, that being the person and the urge, depend on each other to live, but they don't feed off each other. The person needs to kill because the urge is inside them, and the urge needs the person to kill because it is inside them."

"Now you're just trying to confuse me, Art," Artie rattled off sarcastically, hoping to distract the man by diverting his train of thought.

"To put it simply, they kill because if they don't neither of them will survive."

"What happens if you have the urge or whatever and you don't kill?

What happens if you're able to both consciously and unconsciously resist it, huh? What happens then?"

Art's smug, fat-lipped grin telegraphed the answer to Artie before he spoke it.

"It has never happened." The smile broadened to show Art's brown and yellow stained teeth. "No one has ever resisted the urge."

Then his smile shattered into a fit of shrieking laughter.

TWENTY-TWO

ART'S CACKLING NOT ONLY FILLED the small kitchen, it saturated the available space until Artie's ears rang and the laughter took on the impossibly high-pitched whine of a dog whistle. The shrillness was disorienting, and a pin-sized pain in the middle of Artie's brain blossomed to fill his head like the laughter filled the kitchen. Artie's vision blurred and what he was able to make out rattled as if he had been shrunk down and put into a paint mixer.

His knees buckled and Artie took a step back on his left leg to stabilize himself. He squeezed his eyes shut, doing his best to concentrate and remain conscious while attempting to push the pain from his head or, at the very least, endure it for as long as possible; long enough to make a move on the impish man who called himself Art.

When the laughter stopped, the pressure, both in Artie's head and in the kitchen itself, subsided like a slowly deflating balloon. Artie opened his eyes to find he could see somewhat clearly again save for some residual blur around the edges. He didn't wait the extra half a second to think, for fear his window of opportunity would close, and made his move. At least he tried to make his move, but the step back he'd taken put his foot right down in the creeping advancement of the buttery tide rolling in.

He realized this when he pushed off on that foot to leap across the short distance between he and Art, hands outstretched with the intent of wrapping them around the man's moist, fat neck. There was no purchase

76

to be found between his foot and the floor though, and Artie's leg slipped backward, sending him to the floor again but this time by way of a showgirl-style split. Artie was in good shape and limber, but he wasn't ready for it and the electric-hot-pain in his midsection was a telltale sign he'd pulled his groin.

Artie's hands shot to his crotch as he fell over on his side and curled into the fetal position. The pain was too deep inside of him to do anything about, but having his hands clutched within the proximity was still a small comfort. He hoped it would pass or he could fight through it, but the pain was sharp and unyielding. Artie spun halfway around, sending violent waves through the gelatinous, yellow tide splashing in the slick, greasy flavoring. He lost sight of Art when he'd fallen, and despite the pain slithering within his crotch, Artie wanted to get eyes back on the man immediately.

Before he could, the lights went out again, but only for a second, and then they were right back on, then off, then on, then off and on again like a strobe light in slow motion. In the gaps of light between spurts of darkness, Artie saw Art standing right where he had been. His smile was gone, his eyes were narrowed, and he was slowly clapping. The kitchen lights turned on and off each time his hands came together.

TWENTY-THREE

THE CLAPPER WASN'T THE FIRST As Seen On T.V. product, but it was easily the most popular. It was the first thing that came to mind when As Seen On T.V. was brought up in conversation, and not because everybody owned one. Millions upon millions of The Clapper sold in the United States alone, so it would be completely plausible for five out of five people to currently own or to have owned the product.

While it was a great product and has been described by some as 'groundbreaking', The Clapper was not without its flaws. If you clapped, it obeyed, turning on or off depending, but it also performed the function if you coughed or laughed or your dog barked or you closed a door or if someone knocked on the door or if any number of sounds came from your television. People knew this too and still flocked to purchase the 'miracle product' in herds like the mindless bovine they were.

It was that song. It was that goddamn song. The simplicity, the repetition, the fun of clapping along, all of it came together as the perfect ingredients to cast a spell on a public whose minds were easily blown. Like most drugs worth doing, all it took was once and you were hooked. If you managed to escape the lure of The Clapper's siren song and not purchase one, the song would have its revenge by being stuck in your head for days, even weeks.

Few people knew The Clapper has been around since the fifties and served as the product that launched a thousand products for the As Seen

On T.V. brand. In its heyday, The Clapper was all over in every store you went to. You couldn't shake it and you didn't want to.

The Clapper eventually faded into the background slowly, but it never went away and it never will. Thanks to their unique brand of *cradle to the grave marketing* there will always be a new generation to buy it again, and again, and again.

TWENTY-FOUR

ARTIE'S MOTHER BOUGHT A CLAPPER once when he was very young, but she installed it in a room they hardly ever used. It was a guestroom Artie's mother kept in pristine condition, claiming 'You never know when company may stop by'. Artie's mother insisted the door remain closed at all times, so he couldn't even see the magic of The Clapper from the hallway. One night when his Aunt Carol had come to visit, Artie snuck out to the hall after he was supposed to be in bed. He sat outside the door, watching the light sneak out from the space between the bottom of the door and the floor, and he waited.

He waited for over an hour while his aunt no doubt read the Bible or worked on needlepoint, but it was all worth it when Artie heard two soft handclaps. The light vanished, and Artie's obsession was sated for the time being.

He went back to bed but couldn't sleep. He kept playing the memory of the light disappearing from under the door over and over again. The next morning at breakfast, Artie's mother went to check on her sister who hadn't yet stirred since being called down to the table. Seconds later, he heard his mother shriek and call out to god asking 'why' over and over again.

Artie froze, too terrified to run to his mother's aid, and stayed at the table, looking down at his plate for the entire twenty minutes it took for his mother to pull herself together enough to phone for help. Aunt Carol had died sometime during the night with no apparent warning or reason.

A doctor told Artie and his mother an embolism had burst in her brain, killing her instantly, and it was a very sad occurrence but more common than was realized.

Artie's mother couldn't stop crying for what felt like weeks, but all he could do was keep his eyes cast downward while wearing a somber expression. He couldn't bring himself to cry like his mother, not because he was trying to be strong for her, but because he wasn't sad. He knew he was supposed to be, and he tried hard to make himself feel the emotion as he saw it portrayed on people's faces, but he just couldn't. The truth was Artie didn't feel any way in particular about the passing of his aunt. He didn't really think about it in any terms other than it was a thing that happened that day.

What Artie did think about or, rather, obsess over was The Clapper. He couldn't stop thinking about how the last thing his aunt ever did was use The Clapper before she died, and he envied her because of it. He could only hope he would die in the same remarkable fashion one day with the last thing he did being of such great significance.

Sadly, his mother closed up the guestroom permanently in memory of her sister, and not even she would enter the room, let alone operate the lights with or without the aid of technology. At the end of the year, Artie's father moved them to another house all the way across town. It wasn't nearly as nice as their last home, and even worse, his mother didn't bring The Clapper with them.

TWENTY-FIVE

ART **STOPPED HIS PATRONIZING SLOW-CLAP,** leaving what little light there was in the kitchen turned on. The pain in Artie's groin was still roaring through the sensory receptors in his brain, but a sudden second dump of adrenaline, mixed with what little endorphins he still had in his system, helped blunt the sharpest edge of the sensation. This small respite allowed Artie to scoot around on his side and push himself up into a seated position facing Art.

"Are you ready to let me finish," started Art, "or did you want to play slip-n-slide some more? It's up to you, but I'm not sure if it's wise to further aggravate the injury you've given yourself."

Artie's stare pierced the fat man's head, and he envisioned piercing it with something solid and sharp like one of the swords he kept in the 'killing floor' room. He didn't use them often, but sometimes it was fun to role-play being a knight or a samurai.

"I know you're in pain. I told you earlier I am a part of you," continued Art. "I know what you feel, but I choose not to feel it with you, just in case that was your next question."

"Just get to the point of all this," barked Artie, no longer concerned with attempting to keep a level head. "So what, you're the *urge* inside of me that makes me kill? Fine. Who cares? What do you want me to do, stop? Is that what this is all about?"

Art grabbed a handful of popcorn from the bowl, greedily gobbled it, and chewed with his mouth open, letting more of the kernels fall down the front of his shirt than down his throat.

"First of all," Art said through a gulp of half-chewed, white fluff, "I don't *make* you kill. I *let* you, and stopping is the last thing I want. In fact, if anything, I want to increase it both in frequency and quantity."

Artie didn't understand what Art meant by this, but instead of confusion, he only felt angrier. If this person or thing or whatever the hell Art was wanted him to kill more people, why didn't he just say so? Artie could be out right now doing that very thing and enjoying himself while he did it instead of sitting in greasy butter substitute trying to will away the pain buried deep in his crotch.

"Oka-a-a-a-y."

Artie drew out the word, making sure to get his tone under control before going any further. If he could show Art he wasn't upset anymore maybe he might let his guard down long enough for Artie to get the better of him.

"So there was no better way to communicate this to me? I mean, if you're a part of me we should be able to talk about any thing at any time. I'm all for the idea of ramping things up, but we're going to have to do some planning before we—"

"We," interrupted Art, brushing away the popcorn kernels stuck to his chest and stomach. "You see, Artie, that's the problem. It has been *we* this whole time. You and me, me and you, day in and day out for all these years, the two of us have always been a *we*."

Artie didn't like the sudden iciness Art's tone had taken. Artie's mind switched back to high-alert mode as the words raised gooseflesh across his entire body, and he unintentionally reacted to the chill running through him with an involuntary shudder. Artie saw Art smile in reaction to the subtle flinch, interpreting it as a sign of further weakness. Artie almost didn't realize the cold sensation that swept through him served to further dull the pain in his groin to an almost bearable level.

"If you haven't figured it out by now, and I'm sure you have, since you're so smart," continued Art. "It's time to break up the band and go solo. I'm afraid you're hampering my creativity, Artie, and I need to be free to pursue my vision for what I hope to achieve in the future. Unfortunately, you are not a part of that vision."

"So, what? Is that what this is all about?" Artie was no longer trying to speak calmly. "This whole thing is about you wanting to *break up* with me? Fine! Why the hell would I care? I don't need you out there helping or allowing or *urging* me to do anything. I'm sure I'll be fine on my own."

"I'm afraid you once again misunderstand." Art's tone grew impossibly colder and pushed each word into Artie's chest like thin, sharp icicles. "There is no coexistence for you and me. It's one or the other, and by one, I mean me. There can be no other."

The muscles in Artie's midsection tightened, reigniting the blazing pain in his groin as the full realization of what Art was saying sunk in. When Art then produced a rust-covered kitchen utility knife he'd pulled from behind his back, there was no doubt.

TWENTY-SIX

IT TOOK A MOMENT FOR Artie to catch up to what his brain was telling him, like there was some sort of lag between synapses, but he recognized that knife. It wasn't covered in rust, either. It was dried blood. He glanced over Art's shoulder again but already knew what he would see. The knife block resting beneath the shadow of the cupboards above it was now minus one blade.

Artie was familiar with the knife Art was brandishing because it had once been his. When he was younger and making mistakes he'd long since learned from, that knife was his primary weapon. Now he knew it was foolish to pigeonhole himself like that, but this was before he knew any better. Back then Artie was still trying to figure out why he even needed to kill people, but he knew he liked to use the knife.

He enjoyed the reaction the sight of it summoned from the deepest part of his victims' lungs just before he used it to puncture them. The weapon was clunky and left a lot of room for error, but Artie gained some inexplicable joy out of using it, at least for a while.

"Remember this knife? You don't have to answer. I already know you do." Art didn't pause for Artie to answer, but he apparently didn't have to. "Remember the mess it always made and how impractical it was to keep using it over and over? Remember . . . how close you came?"

Art phrased these as questions, but they came off like statements. Artie was starting to understand what Art was getting at. It was becoming clear now what Art meant when he said he *let* Artie kill; he was also letting him get away with it.

"Do you remember the redhead at the mo—"

"Yes, I fucking remember!" Artie fired off, not letting the instigator finish his sentence.

Artie remembered the instance well but hadn't thought about it in years. He wasn't as good at planning and logistics back then, but he hadn't set out with the intention of killing that red-haired girl. Her name was Heather, and he'd been flirting with her at the bar for a few weeks. One night, his labor bore fruit in the form of a heated make-out session in the ladies room that quickly turned into a trip to the motel a few blocks over.

Killing was the furthest thing from Artie's mind that night, and the kind of desire he felt wasn't at all geared toward hurting Heather. Artie had gone into the small office and checked in under a fake name for no other reason than he'd seen it in the movies and it amused him. He was now Cleveland Stefanopolis, and he told the clerk he and his bride-to-be were stopping for the night on their way out to Vegas to get hitched. The clerk didn't even attempt to feign interest as he slid the key to room six across the filthy, Formica-topped counter.

Artie pulled the car around to the parking lot, and a moment later they were in the room, engaged in a whirlwind of lustful passion. From out of nowhere, Artie's thoughts shifted from desire to violence against the girl he'd pined after all these weeks. He did his best to hold them back. He attempted to push them under the prevailing thoughts of sexual conquest, but that only made it worse. The desire to kill became intensely magnified before Artie realized he had blacked out.

An indeterminate amount of time later, he was beside the bed, naked, standing over the nearly unrecognizable corpse of Heather. Blood covered Artie's naked body in various psychedelic patterns of spatter, and there were pools of it on the bed around Heather's body, collected in the folds of the crumpled sheets. His hands and fingers were gashed and cut from all the times the handle, slick with blood, had slipped from his grip. The room was destroyed. More of it was covered in blood than wasn't, and in Artie's carved up hand was the knife. He didn't remember going back out to his car to retrieve it, but he must have, because there it was.

Now the pudgy goblin of Artie's duality stood a few feet away, holding that same knife.

"That was when I learned *I* could make you lose control," Art said. "Or rather, I could take control away from you, and thus, our division began. It was a near imperceptible crack in the bond meant to shackle us to one another eternally, but it was all I needed to begin our separation."

Artie gritted his teeth and began to slowly move his limbs carefully to maneuver himself into a standing position without slipping again or collapsing from the throbbing pain in his midsection. He half-expected Art to pounce before he could make it to his feet and fillet Artie with the knife he'd used on countless others.

Art did not attack though, and instead waited patiently for Artie to find some footing, gain his balance, and finally manage to stand to his feet. Artie didn't expect this exercise in restraint from Art.

"That motel room though," continued Art, "was quite a nasty scene. You made more mistakes with Heather than you had with any other victims leading up to her."

"*I* didn't make those mistakes." Artie's blood pressure spiked and his heartbeat pounded in his head with the resonance of a detuned timpani drum. "You did."

"Of course I did, but you didn't know that then. Hell, I hardly knew it, but I did make sure to take care of you or, rather, us."

"Take care of? It was dumb luck we—*I* got away with that one. The responding officers failed to lock the crime scene down before two maids, the manager, a security guard, and a curious vagrant had all wandered through the room before the detectives had a chance to get there. By the end of it, nothing from the room was admissible in court. They had no evidence, no leads, and *no* suspects. It was a cold case before it ever had a chance to heat up."

Artie curled his fingers into fists, and his fingernails pressed hard enough into his palms to break the skin. He felt blood run down his fingers and remembered what his hands looked like after that night. He remembered how long it took for the cuts to heal and how careful he had to be about showing his hands for weeks. He'd resorted to wearing gloves anytime he left his house, which he kept to a bare minimum.

There were scars, which while faded with time, were still visible if you looked closely. His hands still itched and burned with phantom pains beneath them, depending on how cold it was outside. Artie had since bought an As Seen On T.V. Hand Therapy Lotion-Flow Gloves and Electric Toothbrush, and he was more than pleased with the results. It was well worth the money.

"You're right," Art said through an annoying smirk, "all of those things are true, save for one. The police didn't have a suspect per se, but they did have DNA from the scene that didn't match any of the people who'd aided in contaminating the scene, but unfortunately for them, it also didn't match anyone from the national database. It stores the DNA of all convicted offenders regardless of the severity of the crime. After that, I just needed to make sure the police never had an opportunity to test your DNA ever again, and as you know, they never have."

Artie's anger had reached a level beyond what he'd experienced previously, and his vision narrowed until all he could see was Art's greasy, pimple-covered face wearing an infuriatingly smug expression. Artie didn't want to ask any more questions or hear anything else Art had to say about their supposed life together.

The only thing Artie thought about now was killing Art.

Artie bent his knees and lunged, somehow without slipping in the buttery goop that had claimed the majority of the floor. He wasn't sure what he would do once he got his hands on the squat, slick piece of shit, but Artie was confident he'd figure it out when they connected.

In the moment before Artie's fingers were inches from pay dirt, Art clapped twice, plunging the room into complete darkness. Artie continued well past the point of where he should have made contact, but Art wasn't there anymore.

Artie felt a pinch against his sternum that burned a crooked line down his chest and stomach before he hit the ground.

TWENTY-SEVEN

ARTIE PRIDED HIMSELF ON ALWAYS taking the necessary extra steps to not get caught. Could it really only be because his hand was being guided the whole time by some force working from deep inside of him? It was that night in the motel which prompted Artie to change the way he operated, starting with getting rid of the knife, and then lying low for a good while.

There was no way someone who wasn't Artie would've been able to find where he ditched the knife. Art must truly be a part of him to have been able to retrieve it. Artie's first thought was to throw it into one of the various surrounding bodies of water, but he quickly decided against it. The authorities were sure to dredge and send divers to all of them, and even if they didn't find it on the first pass, they'd find the knife eventually.

Artie would need to take special care with how he disposed of it. He'd need to be creative. The thought suddenly struck him that if the knife didn't exist it could never be found, and he knew exactly what to do.

There was a workshop a few miles from the motel that cut sheets of stainless steel, amongst other metal fabrication work, which was sent to various distributors who supplied oil companies with materials to build machinery. This was long before Artie had discovered the As Seen On T.V. products he would later tinker with, but he'd always been handy.

He was familiar with the shop because he'd picked up a few days of work there a handful of weeks ago. Sometimes, when fabrication shops like this one were bogged down with requests for material, they would hire on temporary help to get through. When the work was done, the temps would be unemployed again, but some of the busy stretches could last weeks or even months.

It was good work when it came along, and decent money for a young man like Artie, so he worked these jobs from time to time. It also helped him keep his hands busy between kills. Gave him something to occupy his mind while he prepared and planned for his next victim. The shop, which was a large warehouse-style metal building, would be locked, but Artie knew a way in.

There were three tall, sliding bay doors kept open during production in the day and chained closed from the inside at night. Artie knew the door in the middle used a longer chain with some slack that allowed the door to be open almost a foot after being locked. Artie had taken note of this security oversight while working there and wondered if it were possible for him to fit through that opening.

The night Artie killed Heather he found out he could indeed slip through. He turned on one of the table saws used to cut smaller sheets of steel and slowly pushed the knife through the blade, cutting it in two. He then cut those two pieces into two more pieces each and split them all again one more time. Artie couldn't cut the pieces any more times without getting his fingers sliced off, but it wouldn't be necessary.

Artie took the eight pieces to a machine on the other end of the shop used to grind small fragments of steel left from custom cut pieces into shavings for scrap. The machine kicked on with a high-pitched whirling drone and sang in off-key shrieks as Artie tossed the eight pieces of knife in one by one. Less than a minute later the weapon he'd used to kill Heather and over a dozen of his early victims was nothing but thin silver slivers mixed with countless other identical thin silver slivers.

In a day, they would be mixed with even more of the same just before being hauled to another mill to be melted. The knife still existed in theory, but it might as well not have. Somehow the knife had been reconstructed by Artie's self-proclaimed 'killing urge', and that urge had just used it to slice Artie open. He folded his arms across his chest and stomach as pain came in hot waves with a slow, intense burn. He struggled to remain conscious, and from somewhere in the darkness came a wet lip-smack. A moment later, Artie's mind shut off and left him swimming in darkness.

TWENTY-EIGHT

THE SOUND RANG SHARP AND defined and woke Artie with the same effect as a bucket of ice water to the face would have. He was disoriented, confused, and for the first few moments of consciousness had no idea where or even who he was. As the shock faded, Artie looked around and realized he was in a familiar place. He was in his bedroom.

Not only that, Artie was in bed and underneath the covers. He stared at the ceiling and ran his fingers along the soft familiarity of the duvet draped across his chest. His head was pounding, and he was having trouble piecing together even one cohesive thought when he tried to sit up. His effort was derailed when a lightning storm of pain in his groin shot electrified bolts up into his stomach and through his chest to his neck.

He'd only managed to raise himself up a few inches before he crashed back down to the mattress seized by the unexpected pain. Artie pulled the covers up and peered beneath before throwing them off completely to confirm what he thought he saw.

A jagged, crooked gash ran from just below Artie's navel all the way up to his clavicle. It was crudely stitched up with what looked like the thick, black thread used to repair upholstery. The wound was red and angry despite the attempt made to repair it, and it wept a thin, clearish-yellow secretion around areas where the stitching wasn't as tight as others.

Through the smokescreen of pain, Artie started to see shadowy objects wandering through his head form into memories. He remembered his confrontation with Art, he remembered his old knife being responsible for the gash on his chest, and when his midsection throbbed, he remembered pulling his groin. Artie lay still in his bed remembering the last two days, and the more he remembered, the more motivated he was to get up.

He knew the pain would be agonizing. He knew he would have to do whatever he could to stay conscious, and he knew if he didn't, he'd be totally fucked whenever Art showed back up. Artie pulled the pillowcase off the pillow his head rested on, folded it twice, and rolled it up as tightly as he could. He put the soft cylinder between his teeth, bit down, and took a deep breath.

Without letting himself think about it, Artie pushed himself up, scooted to the side of the bed, and stood. His plan of trying to move faster than the pain could set in had worked, but now he braced himself for the ensuing tidal wave to catch up. The pain came at full intensity all at once, and Artie howled through the pillowcase, biting hard enough to test the integrity of the material.

His knees buckled, and all he wanted to do was close his eyes and collapse, but he forced himself to focus on something else, something to distract him until he could push through the initial onslaught of pain. Artie saw, in his mind, a familiar place he recognized as the As Seen On T.V. aisle at his local Bloomwalls. The shelves were stocked top to bottom with all completely new products that would blow his mind, test his talents, and streamline his life, but he couldn't see what any of them were, and he never would if he gave up now.

Artie opened his eyes, stood up straight, and used the thought of that aisle to help dull his pain to a semi-manageable level. On his way to the bathroom Artie stopped to look at himself in the full-length mirror. The large wound marred the visage he'd worked so hard to achieve and maintain, but there was no time to mourn.

He somehow managed to get to the shower, but his attempt to clean himself was short-lived. The water hitting his chest reignited the pain, and he turned it back off before his hand left the knob. It took several minutes of focus before he was able to leave the shower and hobble to the sink.

He opened the medicine cabinet and removed a bottle of Vicodin he'd saved from a long-forgotten victim. Another exception to the rule he was glad he made. Artie poured three of the white oval pills into his hand, moved them immediately to his mouth, and dry swallowed without hesitation. It would take a few minutes, but Artie knew the pills would make it much easier to deal with the pain.

While he waited, he gripped both sides of the sink, leaned forward, and stared into the mirror. For the first time, Artie could see similarities to Art in his own features. He didn't notice earlier because of the swollen, cartoonish proportions of Art's face, but the resemblance was there. Artie could see it in his jawline, the shape of his eyes, and even, although it was hard to believe, around the lips.

The thing that called itself Art, the thing claiming to be a part of Artie, the part that *let* him kill, was a grotesquely amplified caricature of himself. Artie stared into his own eyes and saw the reflection become wavy around the edges, letting him know the pills had started to kick in. He pushed off the sink, stood up straight, and tried not to think about the sickening resemblance he'd just noticed.

His balance rocked when he turned, so Artie stood still for a few seconds to get acclimated to the effect the opiate had on his mobility. He settled into the numbing warmth of the drug easily and kept the bottle of pills in his hand until he had a pocket to stuff it into.

The walk back to his bedroom was considerably easier than the journey out, and Artie stepped up to an old, beat up dresser standing chest-high in the far corner. It was oddly out of place compared to the other furniture in Artie's house, but it had belonged to his great grandmother. It was the first and only dresser Artie ever had and was the only thing he made sure to always take when it was time for him to relocate.

Artie yanked the single, half-broken handle on the second drawer from the top and pushed some old t-shirts to the side until he found what he was looking for buried at the bottom. He pulled out a pair of pale-yellow sweatpants and held them out to inspect. He'd only worn them once before when he'd painted the bathroom in his current home. There were still a few dried spots of black paint around the cuffs and down the side of the left leg, but otherwise, they looked brand new.

Artie was staunchly against wearing sweatpants, especially out in public, but in this case he would have to make an exception. He felt when people wore things like sweatpants or gym shorts and similar 'comfort clothing' out of the house, it was not only a sign of laziness but also a signal to others that you'd given up. He believed if you respected yourself you would take the time to make yourself presentable when out amongst people.

The sweatpants were a size too big for Artie, but the elastic waistband hugged just below his hips, which was enough to keep them from retreating to the ground completely. Artie dropped the pants, stepped onto them, and bent his knees slowly to lower himself enough to get hold of the waistband. Since the laceration started below his naval, bending at the waist was out of the question, even with pills to stifle the pain.

Artie tugged the pants up as quickly as the pills-to-pain ratio would allow, suddenly becoming aware of the passage of time. Since he'd come to, Artie had taken forty-five minutes to perform tasks he would typically be done with in ten. His time was finite now.

Despite the piss-poor stitching of his wound there had been no obvious measure taken to clean the injury, and he was sure infection was at that very moment setting in. Artie knew sheer will and Vicodin could only keep the full bite of the pain at bay for so long, and the clock had begun ticking. Artie jammed the bottle of pills into the pocket of the sweatpants but not before choking down one more of the white ovals.

He crossed his bedroom to the door, walking at a normal pace without letting himself even think about pain. He let it melt into a comforting warmth, radiating to his entire body by way of his groin. Hanging off a hook on the back of Artie's bedroom door was the black, zip-up hoodie he wore only for looking inconspicuous at night just in case the mood hit him. It was a size bigger than he actually wore so it would be harder for a potential witness to accurately describe his body type. This was just one of the small precautions Artie took that kept him a free man or maybe it was suggested to him by the tinier, uglier version of himself screaming ideas from his subconscious.

Artie slipped the hoodie on and zipped it to the bottom of his neck. He was worried the back of the zipper against his skin would irritate the wound further, but the contact registered only as a dull vibration. He stepped out into the hall, stopped short, and put his back against the wall. Artie realized the greasy, pig-faced mutant could be in the shadows at the end of the hall waiting to finish him off or, worse, prolong the ordeal by toying with him more.

From the corner of his eye, Artie saw the closed door of the room he called the 'killing floor' and, before he realized, was inching his way down the wall toward it. Seeing the door to the room made him remember how he'd been tricked into killing his neighbor. Artie opened the door just wide enough for him to see the body of Ms. Lancaster strapped to the gurney right where he'd left her.

Artie slammed the door shut, abandoning his attempt at stealth. He didn't know why he looked or what he expected to see. He just needed something else, something outside of himself, to let him know this was all really happening.

Artie gritted his teeth and marched down the hall, his fresh dose of reality having acted like the adrenaline shot to the heart he needed to propel him beyond the pain. If Art was waiting at the end of the hall Artie would rip his fat head off with his bare hands. Even if Artie died in the process he was ready, and it would be worth it. He charged down the hall and stepped out into the living room, ready for a confrontation.

The living room was empty. Artie stood just outside the hall, his breathing heavy with anger, and waited. The room appeared as he'd left it, or at least it did as far as he could remember. It was morning but the heavy cloud coverage plunged the neighborhood into eternal dusk. The shadows in the room cast themselves far and long, using what little light they had to play with.

Artie crossed to the window that faced the garage apartment, not surprised by what he saw. The rain had turned the popcorn into a pasty, white mush that washed down the driveway and clogged all the gutters on the block.

The door was still gone and popcorn filled the entire frame top to bottom. What little still spilled out was turned to mush and swept down the driveway to aid in the disaster currently being created. The same white, fluffy haze filled the glass of the window that faced Artie's. While the rain had let up, it hadn't stopped, and Artie turned from the window, fighting against the warm fuzz in his brain to devise a plan.

He walked to the kitchen but stopped when he crossed the shorter hall leading to the front door. The door was open half an inch, but more alarming was the stack of new As Seen On T.V. products Artie had purchased the day his life was changed for the worse were gone. He knew he had more important things to worry about, but he hadn't even had the chance to open any of them. His rage intensified. Artie took this as a personal slap in the face, an insult.

Artie barreled to the door, slammed it closed, and turned to the end table by the door where he kept his keys. There were keys there but they weren't his, and he snatched them up to take a closer look. The keychain was an orange oval with the word Fiero etched into the hard plastic. Along with the keys, a plastic rectangle dangled from the ring. It was a Bloomwalls Loyalty Discount card, and it was soaked with blood.

TWENTY-NINE

ARTIE WENT TO THE GARAGE and his car was gone, which he anticipated would be the case. He reached into the right pocket of his sweatpants for the bottle of pills, shook two more into his mouth, and swallowed before returning them to their deep, cotton cradle.

From his left pocket Artie produced the keys to the Fiero. He wiped them against his pants as he pressed the button on the wall to activate the automatic garage door opener. Artie didn't bother with an umbrella, raincoat, or even a poncho as he made his way down the driveway. The house shoes he'd slipped on were soaked and soggy and filthy popcorn mush clung to the outsides of them up to his ankle.

As he neared the end of the driveway, Artie saw the mayhem the wet popcorn had caused to the street's drainage system. The water in the street was just below the doors of the bright orange monstrosity of a car. Artie remembered hearing how Fieros used to spontaneously catch fire when he was a kid, and for some reason it made the car that much more enticing to him. He never did get one, which is why it made perfect sense that Art be driving one. Now the sight of it turned his stomach.

Artie stepped out into the water rushing down the street, surprised at the strength of the current. It would only get stronger as the water rose, which was happening at a rapid pace. He felt it sneaking up his shins with each step toward the door, and he held the keys out as far as his arm would reach. Artie plunged the key into the silver-ringed circle just as the water reached the seam of the door.

He struggled, fighting against the rising water as it rushed in through the opening. When he managed to open the door wide enough, he slid through and pulled it shut as he fell into the driver seat. His feet splashed in the several inches of water on the floorboard, and he kicked around to find the pedals.

When his foot found the clutch he mashed it down while twisting the key into the side of the steering column. The engine sputtered and coughed, but refused to turn over. Artie tried again, now able to feel the water getting deeper at his feet, but the car hacked louder, mocking him and his attempt. He turned the key one last time, screaming with rage as he did. A black cloud belched from the tailpipe of the car like a chemical plant smokestack, and the engine begrudgingly came to life. The car squealed like a dying animal as Artie slammed the gearshift into first and stomped the gas while easing up on the clutch.

The Fiero pulled away from the curb slowly despite Artie having the gas pedal to the floor, and the engine coughed, threatening to die again. He shifted into second and pressed the accelerator slowly this time as he maneuvered the car to the center of the street where the water wasn't as high. The lack of power steering combined with the depth of water made it nearly impossible to turn the wheel, and Artie struggled to make it bow to his will.

He heard an audible, wet pop come from beneath his hoodie, followed by a throbbing pressure in the center of his chest. One of the stitches had broken under the strain of turning the wheel, and thick, sour-smelling ooze escaped, leaving a stinging trail as it slowly ventured down past his stomach to soak into the bottom of his sweatshirt.

Once Artie was out of the deepest part of the water, the car was able to pick up speed, and there was no need for him to turn the wheel again for three blocks. He hoped the water would have receded by the time he'd made it that far, but the flooding was worse than he thought.

Every storm drain he passed was jammed tight with popcorn mush and the water climbed, unable to escape to the sewer below. It had reached the top of the curb and waves created by the forward momentum of the Fiero pushed water up into the lawns Artie drove past. If the rain didn't let up, the water would start making its way into the houses, his included, but Artie didn't imagine he'd be staying there much longer.

Artie remembered there being a lot of popcorn but had no idea enough escaped the small garage apartment to clog drains for miles. The street was flooded all the way to the main four-way-stop intersection where the water finally had a place to go. Artie had gotten the Fiero to rumble its way there, but when he made the left turn he could see the respite would be short-lived.

These drains weren't clogged, but overflowing and pushing the water out, unable to accept anymore. The overabundance of runoff from Artie's street surged ahead, looking for a way to escape underground with no other choice but to keep rushing on until a clear route could be found.

The water rose by the second but wasn't near as deep as it was on Artie's street, and he took advantage by shifting into higher gears while pushing the gas pedal to the bottom of the puddle the floorboard had become. The Fiero surprisingly had some pickup to it when it wasn't in water up to its hood. Artie navigated carefully, blowing through the three stop signs on his way to the upcoming traffic light.

He yanked hard at the wheel to turn onto the street that would take him to Bloomwalls and, if his hunch was correct, to Art as well. Artie felt the stitches in his chest strain as his slashed flesh pulled apart from the effort needed to turn the wheel. He let up halfway through the turn to reduce the tension on the stitches, allowing them to continue on with their job.

All Artie had to do was make it the three quarters of a mile down the road to the Bloomwalls and wrap his hands around the fat, sweaty neck of his tormentor. After that, he didn't care what happened. Artie could split down the middle and fall as two separate pieces while his intestines and other organs flopped to the ground like human slop being thrown into a pigpen for all he cared.

The rain came down progressively harder the closer Artie got to the Bloomwalls until he might as well have been driving underwater for all he could see through the windshield. He had to guess where to make the turn into the parking lot, and he guessed wrong. The front end of the

Fiero dipped down suddenly, and stopped.

THIRTY

THE CAR HAD HIT THE bottom of the four-foot deep drainage ditch that ran along the road. He had missed the driveway by a dozen feet, and now the Fiero sat at a forty-five degree angle, the engine completely submerged. Artie hadn't thought to buckle up before he left, being more concerned with getting the car started and out of the quickly rising water.

He wasn't going very fast but the jolt still pressed his chest into the steering wheel, adding a fresh dose of fire to a pain too intense for the pills in his system to extinguish. Artie let out an anguished groan as the pain got on top of him again like it was seeking vengeance for having been stifled by the opiates. His vision went black around the edges before complete darkness overtook it.

Artie became aware of a flickering light like that of a flame, but he couldn't tell where it was coming from. The flicker grew brighter, and Artie's feet started to burn. There was no doubt where the fire was now. A crackling followed, but not like what you'd hear from logs on a campfire. It was less of a crackle and more of a pop, and with each pop Artie felt a chunk of flesh separate from his legs, feet, and knees, birthing a unique level of pain to his system with each tiny burst.

A fluffy, white, lightly buttered popcorn kernel leapt in Artie's face, and he looked down to confirm what he already knew. He was standing in a fire while his body exploded into pre-buttered, unsalted popcorn, one kernel at a time.

Artie forced himself awake, breaking free of the terrible vision before it had a chance to go any further. He knew he had only been out for a second or two because water was only just starting to come in through the dashboard. He rolled down the window, pulled himself halfway out into the driving rain, and paused to clutch at his pocket for the pill bottle.

He wrestled it from his soaked sweatpants, shook the bottle, and then seamlessly popped off the childproof lid with one hand. Artie estimated there were four or five more Vicodin, by the sound of it, and he brought the bottle to his lips and tilted it into his mouth. He dry swallowed what felt more like six or seven pills although he could have had a mouthful of water by tilting his head back had he chosen to. Artie wasn't thinking survival anymore; he just wanted to make it long enough to destroy the grotesque character claiming to be the embodiment of what made him kill.

The water in the ditch was six inches shy of Artie's waist, and he pulled himself up the slick, grassy slant to the parking lot holding his oversized, waterlogged pants up with one hand, his slippers lost somewhere along the way. When he was out of the ditch, Artie pulled hard on the drawstrings of the sweatpants and cinched them tight with a double knot despite the waistband digging further into his wound. The hooded sweatshirt clung close to Artie's body, pulled down by the weight of the water it absorbed. The sensation somehow soothed the blaze in his chest.

Artie turned to face the store. On any other day he could have made it to Bloomwalls in less than five minutes, but today the short trip was rife with danger that threatened his life more than once. The sky behind the store ignited into crooked bolts of free-range electricity that bent and crisscrossed like the gnarled fingers of an ancient witch. On the heels of the lightning a long and low thunderclap dropped slowly from the sky like it was riding down a waterfall of melting tar. There was no urgency in its decay.

If it was true what he'd heard about counting the seconds between lightning and thunder to see how many miles away the storm was, then it was directly on top of him. Artie began the walk across the parking lot as the back and forth between lightning and thunder continued like the two were having a heated debate.

He was halfway across the parking lot but Artie could see through the driving sheets of rain that the glass door was smeared with blood. Strewn across the sidewalk around the door were boxes that had been torn apart, their contents smashed and soaked, rendered useless by rage and the elements. They were the remains of the new As Seen On T.V. products Artie had purchased two days ago. He never got the chance to unlock their hidden magic, have them whisper sweet secrets in his ear, and now he never would. Artie pulled up his soaked sweatpants and quickened his pace.

Art was here.

THIRTY-ONE

ON ANY OTHER DAY IT would have been the most elaborate Halloween display Donna and the rest of the Bloomwalls employees had ever assembled. Not on this day though, and Halloween was still months away. If what Artie saw *had* been props the cost of the display would have been astronomical, but the realism, the attention to detail, even the replicated stench of death, would've made it worth every single penny.

What Artie had walked into was a very real house of horror. The amount of blood was comically excessive. There was so much it was hard to imagine all of it being real. Artie was no stranger to blood, but something about what he was seeing created a theatric feeling both dark and chilling.

The buzz from the glowing fluorescent tubes in the ceiling was noticeably louder, and scattered banks of light flickered throughout the store. He was still standing just inside the door, taking in the scene but mostly looking for Art. He took a step and the slap of his bare foot against the filthy tile was also louder than it should have been. Artie paused and realized why the lights and his footfalls sounded so amplified.

The store was silent, not just quiet, but a vacuously eerie silence like a two-hundred-pound, invisible blanket had been dropped on the store to prevent every last decibel from escaping its smothering. His slow and cautious steps fell like cannon fire, and he kept his head on a swivel to avoid ambush but only caught glimpses of gore down every aisle he passed.

The first face he saw—at least what was left of it—Artie recognized as Donna. Half her face had been messily cut away, but the half that was left held the unmistakable apathy of the cashier as if she couldn't be bothered by her own death. She was down on her knees, only her knees were bent forward, and something against her back was keeping her propped up.

When he got closer, Artie could see a cash register drawer had been rammed into her back in such a way that kept Donna from falling over. The drawer had gone into her back and most of the way through her slim midsection. Enough of it came out of her stomach for Artie to have easily made change for a dollar as long as he didn't mind digging through the half-digested contents of Donna's small intestine for his quarters.

Artie could tell this hadn't been the way her body happened to fall after being delivered the killing blow. It had been staged this way, but now he knew why. Donna's left arm hung slack at her side, one of her favorite fashion magazines still clutched in her hand like a wink to an audience made only of Artie. Her right arm was extended, held out and in place by being rested on a stack of boxes containing cheap mixed chocolates typically purchased in haste for a forgotten anniversary.

Donna's finger hung limp from her swollen hand, but it was clear to Artie it was pointing in the direction he was supposed to go, indicating his nightmarish scavenger hunt continued on. Also, it was the only finger left on Donna's hand, as the others, including the thumb, had been bitten off, from the looks of it. The irony of Donna's middle finger left pointing the way was not lost on Artie. His bare feet were soaked and stained red by the still growing puddle of blood around Donna. The crimson tracks Artie left behind as he headed down the aisle served only to amplify the horror show aesthetic.

The aisle was littered with the paper towels, napkins, and other assorted paper products usually neatly arranged on the shelves. The now mostly empty shelves down the right side of the aisle were dripping red like they'd been painted carelessly with an oversaturated brush.

At the other end of the aisle lay a body crumpled in a way that looked like bones had to be removed to achieve its current state. Chunks of skin and muscle clung to and dangled from shelves, having been deposited there when the man was scraped back and forth across the front edges again and again, over and over.

Some of the longer pieces of skin hung like greasy strips of flypaper dappled with coarse, black hairs. Others looked like chewed bubblegum had been stuck to the shelves at random by some obstinate child going through a rebellious stage. Artie wasn't bothered by the blood or pieces of the man or even the shards of shattered teeth he'd stepped on. What bothered him was the reckless way these killings had been so carelessly executed.

These were total rage-killings, committed for seemingly no reason. Artie was no saint, but he attempted to balance his misdeeds with justification. He was a professional or at least considered himself one, and what he was seeing in the store was the work of a bush league amateur. What was most perplexing and somewhat troubling to Artie was that if Art killed these people and if he was a part of Artie, *the* part that made him a killer, then why would he do this? Not the actual killing but the way in which he did it with barbaric rage and no demure, no forethought and certainly no second thought.

Artie was never this sloppy and brazen, even with his first victims when he actually still felt the true angst and rage that accompany youth. Art told him the reason Artie remained a free man was due only to his influence, which included all the beneficial habits he'd developed and refined over the years. Why would Art himself not be careful?

Because I don't have to.

Artie heard the unmistakable voice of Art in his head and wondered if it had been there all along. What if he could hear it now because he was actually tuned in to it? Tuned in to Art. Ripples of fear radiated from Artie's chest and threatened his confidence, but he refocused to keep them from turning into full-blown waves of panic. The pills helped with that too.

Artie stood over the dead employee at the end of the aisle. To see the contorted mess was another helpful clue, pointing him in the 'right' direction. The man was on his back with his left leg straight up to the ceiling. His right arm had been pulled, stretched, and tied to the leg at mid-calf, which kept it in position.

When Artie originally saw the body from the other end of the aisle, he suspected bones had to be missing for it to be 'arranged' the way it was. Now, up close, he saw he was partially right. The bones hadn't been removed from the body but pulverized into calcium-rich pebbles that remained encased within the original, meat-tube packaging. This was why Art was able to actually tie one limb to the other like the corpse was a life-sized Stretch Armstrong doll.

The right leg was bent at the knee and pulled up to his chest. The ankle had been broken and the foot spun to face the opposite way it was meant to. The dead man's right arm, which also resembled that of a rubber, putty-filled doll, was pulled tight enough to make the skin translucent, like a bat wing, and equally as veiny and grotesque. The arm was tied to the broken, backward foot where, with the elegant touch of a balloon animal aficionado, the jellyfish-like, boneless fingers had been woven and twisted to form an arrow indicating Artie turn left down the center aisle.

He studied the man's bashed and contorted figure, finding a certain intriguing beauty in the arrangement of his body. Artie didn't really know any of the Bloomwalls employees outside of Donna, but he wouldn't have been able to recognize this one even if he did. The man's face was shredded pulp, but it couldn't have gotten as mangled as it was from only being slammed into the edge of the shelving,

The image of a fang-mouthed Art flashed in his mind, and Artie could picture him hunched over, chewing the man's face to minced meat. The two wide, lidless eyes fixed in a terrified stare was the only reminder the pile of ground chuck next to Artie's foot used to be someone's face.

Artie bent down and straightened the man's official Bloomwalls puke-green vest with orange piping so he could see the employee's nametag. His name was Karl with a 'K', and according to the title beneath it, he was the assistant manager. Artie vaguely remembered being helped by Karl one day and vacillated on the idea of killing him then but decided against it since he still had a victim at the house locked in the 'killing floor' he was still working on.

Artie stepped over the morbid sculpture formerly known as Karl and hung a left down the center aisle. If he hadn't been stoned into utter numbness Artie would have felt the shattered slivers of Karl's teeth slide farther into the bottoms of his feet with each step. He could see the next human directional display four aisles down indicating for him to turn right, which would put him in the As Seen On T.V. aisle.

He walked slowly, partially from his excessive opiate intake but mostly to look down the aisles he'd glimpsed on his way in. The pills were starting to get on top of Artie, but he didn't have far to go, and he didn't intend for what was going to happen when he got there to take long. About halfway down the center of the first aisle was a clear and unobstructed view of an unfortunate looking vagina.

The person it belonged to was bent over the front of a shopping cart with her face down in a load of bloody groceries, so it took Artie a second to realize who it was. Well, he didn't really *know* who it was, but he did know it was one of the blue-hairs that stalked Bloomwalls on a daily basis.

Artie took a few steps down the aisle to get a better look and saw the head down in the basket was on backward, the death caused by a clean snap of the neck. The pants of her purple tracksuit had been pulled down to her white, non-descript old lady shoes to expose the ancient and frightening genitalia. Silver hair engulfed the majority of the region and continued its way up the crack of her ass, bristling out like a rotating brush in an automatic carwash. The labia hung down four or five inches lower than it should have been and were as equally covered in curly, white hair. Artie thought they looked like a pair of sideburns waiting for a face to grow between them.

He didn't spend much more time examining the old woman's hair-ensconced nether region and continued on his way, afraid her bush would all of a sudden grab and pull him into the woman's corpse via her dry, mangled hole. The stink wafting out of it was bad enough to rival death, and it stuck in Artie's nose.

The next two aisles also included dead blue-hairs, but the bodies weren't displayed in provocative or offensive ways. The two aisles were scenes of frenzied, high-throttle violence. There were multiple bodies of old women in each aisle, but it was impossible to tell how many since they were stacked together in two piles. Blood was still pushing its way out from beneath both piles, which explained the excessive amount of the stuff at the front of the store.

Various items from the surrounding shelves had spilled out across the aisles, creating small, dammed off areas where blood had been allowed to pool up to three inches. If Artie had had the time or desire to investigate the piles of bodies he would have found it quite an ingenious configuration. They were in a pile, but the corpses had each been stacked facing down and with their heads all tilted slightly toward the floor. Their necks had all been broken and throats slit so blood would continue to drain until they were all empty meat-sacks.

Artie approached the body beckoning him to enter an aisle he was very familiar with. This was another employee Artie didn't know, but the nametag hanging from his now blood-spattered, signature Bloomwalls vest said Tom, with the 'o' made to look like a smiley face. He doubted Tom would see the whimsy in him being turned into a limbless torso with his arms sticking out of his ribcage, emphatically pointing down the aisle to Artie's destiny.

The aisle usually brought on an intoxicating serotonin dump with the accompanying endorphin rush, but he had a feeling the association was about to be damaged beyond repair. Whatever waited in the As Seen On T.V. aisle for Artie he knew would not invoke a similar feeling, and whatever happened, he wasn't coming back.

THIRTY-TWO

THE **BANK OF LIGHTS OVER** the As Seen On T.V. aisle was among those flickering, and any illumination they did provide was dim and useless. Surprisingly, the aisle was free of blood and carnage, the only area in the entire store spared from even a drop. Artie hadn't expected to round the corner and find Art sitting on a throne of skulls drinking the blood of old women from a chalice, but it wouldn't surprise him. The odd thing about the aisle, aside from it *not* being the location of violent murder, was that the shelves were all empty. Well, mostly empty.

The large area in the middle where the products Artie obsessed over were usually displayed was barren except for a single box. He stepped into the aisle and paused, waiting for that 'something' he was looking for earlier to happen, but it did not. Artie's ears popped, and he felt a slight change in air pressure when he took another step toward the box.

Artie could see the famously recognizable As Seen On T.V. logo on one side, but the side of the box picturing the product was turned away from him. He took another step and felt the air grow denser, like it was pushing him back. He suddenly realized there was no invisible force working to slow his forward momentum. It was the pills. He may have numbed himself from the sting but now that the adrenaline surge keeping him upright was gone, his gland depleted.

The overwhelming urge to lie down in the aisle, close his eyes, and enjoy a sleep he would never wake up from was hard to resist as an invisible weight pushed down, coaxing him to the floor. He stumbled forward and fell to one knee, his will too strong to go down all the way. Artie reached out and grabbed one of the empty shelves and pulled himself back to his feet. The strain caused a spark in his chest to reignite the kindling of pain, dull and warm at first, but quickly growing with intensity.

The pain fought hard to break through the opiate barrier, and if Artie didn't pass out from the pills, the pain would make sure he did. He didn't understand what Art was waiting for to confront him? Surely he had something more interesting for Artie in store other than just letting him pass out and die, but maybe he didn't? Maybe Artie was a dead man all along and Art was using this game to prolong his suffering? Was the climax Artie had powered through to get to in fact the absence of a climax entirely?

The pain in his chest, while becoming increasingly problematic, cut through the Vicodin fog around his brain and reinvigorated Artie's sense of urgency. He grabbed at the box and spun it toward him, ignoring the itch clawing at the inside of his half-stitched gash. He stared at the picture on the box, not sure of what to think as a thousand needle-pricks raced along the raw edges of the wound, making the itch harder to ignore.

Words across the top proudly declared the contents to be the Hair Straightener/Degreaser/Popcorn Maker combo that had eluded Artie on his last shopping excursion. He turned the box around again and again like he expected it to become something else, but nothing changed. Artie unconsciously brought his hand to his chest to scratch at what felt like a centipede with dagger-feet climbing down his crooked stitches but caught himself before he made contact, opting to unzip the hoodie instead.

The added weight made it easy for Artie to shrug out of the wet, oversized sweatshirt, but exposing his chest to the open air only made the wound angry and hot. He refused to look down but could feel heat radiating up at his face, the kind of heat that accompanies infection. Wet warmth wound winding paths from where the wound had begun to weep down into the front of his waistband.

Artie ripped at the top of the box, struggling to slip his fingers beneath the tape that sealed it, until he discovered one of the edges folded up. He pinched the tiny fold between his thumb and forefinger and pulled, successfully bringing the rest of the tape with it. He peeled slowly, unintentionally, which only heaped more weight atop the already insurmountable pressure in the room. He pulled one of the cardboard flaps open and a few white, foam packing peanuts stuck to the underside fell onto the shelf beside the box.

Artie ripped the other flap open, revealing more packing peanuts beneath, only they weren't packing peanuts; they were kernels of yellow-dusted popcorn. He went to plunge his hand in but buckled when something twisted in his stomach. His mouth salivated in a way that preceded vomiting, but a mass above Artie's sternum was blocking the contents of his stomach from reaching his throat.

The mass swelled within him rapidly, and something sharp stabbed Artie through the center of it. He stumbled back from the shelf, thinking he'd sprung a trap hidden within the box that ran something sharp into his midsection, but when he looked down, he found that wasn't the case. There was a swollen mass growing from his chest and the stabbing occurred just below it but not from a secret sabotage buried beneath stale popcorn.

There was a knife in Artie's stomach, only, the pointed end was facing out, and the blade was growing. He had been stabbed from the inside out.

THIRTY-THREE

ARTIE WATCHED THE KNIFE BEING pushed out from inside of him pause before it began to work its way up, slicing along the same ragged gash Art had given him. The subpar stitches were popped easily by the blade, allowing his body to purge the green and yellow, poisonous ooze in larger quantities. Artie could only watch, his arms bent in toward the savage re-opening of the wound, hands hovering inches away, fingers paralyzed and gnarled.

The blade continued slicing upward, having to saw at the stitches it snagged on. Artie's chest continued to swell and, as the knife reached the bottom of the mass, part of his pink, slick intestine pushed out and to the side of the opening. When it kept pulling at the parted flesh, Artie blinked away tears to see it wasn't a piece of his viscera escaping. It was a hand.

The knife stopped slicing and sawing, but he wasn't as concerned about it as he had been a second earlier. Fingers attached to the hand gripped the parted curtain of flesh and pulled to widen the opening for what was to follow. Next came a gore-slicked foot followed by another with the attached legs in tow like Artie was giving birth to slick, doughy pythons.

His chest burst apart at the sternum, and his ribs pushed off to either side as a fat, familiar, oddly shaped head pushed its way through. Artie fell on his back as Art stepped out from inside him. He was naked and slimy with a suicide cocktail of bodily fluids. His curly hair was pressed down against his head and face, and in his left hand, he was holding Artie's knife.

Artie gasped for breaths like they were wisps of smoke gone rogue from a quickly burning joint. Movement below Artie's chin mimicked each attempt, and he glanced down to see exposed lungs rising and falling from the small amount of air his shallow breaths allowed. One of them hung off the right side of his ruptured chest, having been displaced by Art during his macabre exit. The gash was torn open wide, allowing him to see his organs, most of which were squashed and torn from having a small person cut their way out of his body.

None of it made any sense, yet here Artie was splayed open like a Russian nesting doll, pulled apart and cast aside for the smaller, fatter reward that lie within. Art stood to the side of Artie, staring down at him. Blood and mucus dripped from his short, squat body like crocodile tears of tapioca. A smile parted the sludge on Art's face, and his yellow teeth stood out like the beacon atop a lighthouse. Artie felt cold and hot simultaneously and wandered if his victims felt the same in their final moments. It wasn't altogether unpleasant.

"You can't talk so don't bother to ask any more pathetic questions like *why*." Art's voice had taken on another new quality. In addition to having lowered an octave or two since Artie's first interaction with him at the window, there was a biting rasp to it as well. The affectation enhanced an overall sinister quality Artie was only now realizing was always there.

"I've already explained that to you as much as I care to," he continued. "In case you haven't figured it out from the metaphor of me cutting myself out of you, that's exactly what I've done."

Metaphor? Did that mean everything Artie went through since he woke up with his chest crudely sewn together wasn't necessary? It was all just a farewell fuck you from the man who'd gotten the better of him?

"I have good news though," Art said, pacing beside the splayed carcass he'd turned Artie into. "It turns out I *don't* have to kill you in order to exist separately from you. Isn't that great?"

Great? Artie could feel the sensation of life evacuating by the second, like thousands of tiny escape pods rocketing out from the exploding starship of his dying form. He was as good as dead, and Art was just trying to prolong Artie's anguish in his final moments.

"If you're worried about all . . . that," Art gestured at the splayed gash he'd just stepped out of as if it were a minor abrasion. "Well, I'm going to fix all that, so don't you worry."

Artie replied with a bloody cough that sprayed a mist of moist micro-rubies into the air around him.

"I said you wouldn't be able to speak," Art paused to look down at Artie again. "Trust me. If you could see your insides from where I was standing . . . well, that doesn't really matter now. I know that you know you're as good as dead, and walking away to let you pass peacefully . . . as peacefully as you can in your current state, would be the easiest thing for both of us, but easy is never fun. I want to make this fun."

Artie was fading. Darkness crept in from all sides, narrowing his field of vision down to pinprick-sized holes. He could still hear Art although the words sounded far away and echoed as if he was talking to him from deep inside a cave. He tried to stop listening, relax, and just let go, but something kept him hanging on. Something wouldn't let him go.

"By fun, I mean fun for me, of course," Art continued, "but the silver lining for you, my friend, is life. You get to live, and I, too, get to exist now separate from you, which I feel personally is a win for both of us."

What Artie was able to see within his limited vision began to swirl and fade in and out like a lazy strobe light. It took a few seconds for him to focus enough to see eyes close to his staring down through him. Art had knelt and was bent over so his face was inches from Artie's.

"Bye bye, Artie," Art said in the original, high-pitched, annoying voice he'd spoken in when the two first met. "I'd say I'll miss you, but we both know that's not true."

Artie's final bit of strength diverted to his irises, which shifted and focused on a pair of plump, chapped, blood-splotched lips, twitching in a familiar way. His vision gave out, plunging him into darkness a moment before he heard the sound. The wet, disgusting, saliva-drenched sound that had plagued his dreams for so long was all the while a signal, a countdown of sorts, to let Artie know his time was limited. Now he understood. It was Art's way of telling Artie he was coming, and soon there would be no Artie to speak of. There would only be Art.

A tremendous relief washed over Artie's consciousness as he was able to mercifully allow what he assumed was death to take him. The rotating hot and cold flashes had ceased, and he melted into numbness. What followed was not a falling or rising sensation or any kind of sensation at all. There was just nothing, and Artie was gone.

THIRTY-FOUR

IT STARTED AS A TINGLE. The sensation was soft, at first, and almost comforting before quickly shifting into the intensity of an electrical shock. The shock pulsed, rising and falling like a heartbeat until it exploded into a blue and white light that roused Artie back from the abyss. It was like he was being reborn or, at the very least, rebuilt.

Artie could feel each part of his body vibrate one at a time like various components of a computer coming back online after being rebooted. When his brain received the tingle, Artie was able to remember, and images flashed through his mind he didn't understand. He saw a drop of blood on his immaculately clean floor. He saw a popcorn-filled room, and he saw himself kill the woman who lived next door, only he didn't know why.

He saw Bloomwalls, his precious As Seen On T.V. product collection, and then he saw the fat, ugly face of a squat, troll-like ghoul, which brought it all back. The electric tingle was gone, and Artie could feel his body and limbs like he used to. Something cold and wet and sticky was clutched tightly in his right hand, and without thinking about if he was able to or not, Artie opened his eyes.

The last thing he could glean from his fuzzy, recovered memories was being in Bloomwalls, sliced open from groin to neck, and lying on his back like a freshly gutted fish thrown to the bottom of the boat. He was most certainly not in that position anymore. Artie looked around, trying to get his bearings, trying to get a handle on where he was and what was happening.

He scanned the walls of the low-lit room he was in and saw framed, generic prints of random and boring scenery. Artie could not yet tell what the random red splotches across the pictures were. He held his right hand up in front of him to see he was tightly clutching a blood-slicked knife.

His knife.

The pieces were coming together, and the realization of where he was set in, casting an inky, black shadow across his consciousness. He was in a motel room, *the* motel room. Artie looked down, already knowing what he'd see, but he couldn't help himself. On the bed in front of him was the viciously mutilated body of Heather.

Now Artie knew the red splotches were blood, and it was everywhere. On the walls, the ceiling, the bed, of course, and all over him. He was back at the exact moment Art told him he'd begun to intervene. All the while, the so-called 'help' he gave Artie was self-serving to make Art stronger, so he could separate the two of them.

Another thought darkened Artie's mind in that moment. Art had let him live, that much was true, but now he wished he was dead. There was no mistaking Art was no longer a part of Artie now, as he could feel the emptiness the killing urge had once occupied, which meant—

The door to the room crashed open before Artie could finish his thought, but he wasn't surprised. Two police officers with guns drawn and trained on him filled the space the door had been occupying.

"Freeze!" one of them yelled. "Drop the knife and put your hands on your . . . oh Christ."

The officer was cut short when he glanced down at the butchered body on the bed, but he recovered quickly.

". . . your hands on your head, goddammit! And drop the knife now!"

The click of the hammer being pulled back on the officer's revolver punctuated the seriousness of his request, and Artie opened his fingers, letting the knife fall to the blood-soaked carpet at his feet. He put his hands on his head and went to his knees while sirens wailed their approaching presence in the background.

One of the officers had come in, cuffed Artie's hands behind his back, and pulled him to his feet. Artie took in the scene with a new clarity and saw the awful mess he'd made of the young woman he supposed he'd always intended to kill. Despite the tremendous amount of blood and viscera coating the room, Artie realized something was off.

The officer held Artie by the cuffs with one hand and jammed the barrel of the revolver into his back with the other as he pushed him toward the door, but Artie stopped a few steps from the egress.

"Keep movin'," barked the officer.

"Do you smell that?" Artie asked, sniffing at the air.

"Smell what?" The officer shoved him, but Artie held his position.

"Popcorn," Artie said. "It smells like popcorn."

Acknowledgments

Special thanks to that goddamn jingle for *The Clapper*. You saved more lives than you'll ever know.

John Wayne Comunale lives in Houston Texas to prepare himself for the heat in Hell. He is the author of *Porn Star Retirement Plan*, *Charge Land, Aunt Poster, John Wayne Lied to You, Death Pacts and Left-Hand Paths,* and *Scummer.* He tours with the punk rock disaster, johnwayneisdead. John Wayne is an American actor who died in 1979.

Other Grindhouse Press Titles

Made in the USA
Middletown, DE
19 September 2021

48621991R00080